"Don't y[...]
before you fall asleep?"

"Too late," Chance mumbled, pulling Julia closer on the bed. As he shifted his booted leg over hers, there was the distinct sound of ripping cloth. "Damn."

"Damn is right," she confirmed. "That was a Pratesi sheet you just put your foot through."

"I just put that *spur* through," he wryly corrected. More tearing was heard before he finally untangled his feet. "Pra—*what?*"

"Pratesi," she repeated. "Good linen. Roughly the price of a month's rent."

"Ouch." He yanked off his boots. Reaching for his belt buckle, he asked, "New York or Pennsylvania rent?"

Grinning, she sat up to help him out of his jeans. "New York. Or four root canals with crowns, in your lingo."

"Double ouch. No more spurs in the bedsheets for us!"

Bestselling author **Sheryl Danson** always wanted to write about a cowboy. "I'm a sucker for a hunk in jeans, boots and Stetson," she says with a grin. Her hero Chance is a wonderful cowboy— who also happens to be a dentist! Men in that profession can be just as romantic, Sheryl points out. And we agree. A native of Pennsylvania, this delightful, talented author is hard at work on her next Temptation novel.

Books by Sheryl Danson

HARLEQUIN TEMPTATION

Don't miss any of our special offers. Write to us at the following address for information on our newest releases.

Harlequin Reader Service
U.S.: 3010 Walden Ave., P.O. Box 1325, Buffalo, NY 14269
Canadian: P.O. Box 609, Fort Erie, Ont. L2A 5X3

THE RANGER MAN
SHERYL DANSON

Harlequin Books

TORONTO • NEW YORK • LONDON
AMSTERDAM • PARIS • SYDNEY • HAMBURG
STOCKHOLM • ATHENS • TOKYO • MILAN
MADRID • WARSAW • BUDAPEST • AUCKLAND

For BB, because Beechnut Coffee tastes better black,
it's better every way

ISBN 0-373-25603-5

THE RANGER MAN

Copyright © 1994 by Sheryl McDanel Munson.

Printed in U.S.A.

HE WAS absolutely perfect.

Julia Adams accorded him that distinction the very instant she saw him in the produce aisle, standing next to the pyramid of iceberg lettuce. He was tall and lean, a credit to his jeans, with a lush crop of sun-bleached hair that made her fingers itch to touch it. If he were any more perfect, he would have been a figment of her imagination.

When he chose a head of lettuce, tossed it into his cart and wheeled around the corner toward canned goods, Julia rushed to follow, consigning her selection of oranges to oblivion. She could always find more oranges; he, on the other hand, was one of a kind, as rare these days as Siberian white tigers. She should know. She'd been searching for him for six long months, during which she'd learned that tracking the absolutely perfect man was neither a quick nor easy undertaking. Now that she'd finally found him, she wasn't about to let him get away.

She stalked him down the canned-goods aisle, keeping her distance and doing her best to appear as if she weren't following him. Now and then, she plucked random cans and boxes off the shelves and threw them into her buggy. Unknowingly, she managed to accumulate several lifetimes' supplies of sardines, pickled beets, and lima beans along the way.

She continued her pursuit up and down the aisles, past meat and pet foods and paper products. Beef tripe, steak-and-kidney cat food, and cartoon-character-emblazoned party plates all found their way into her buggy, none wanted nor needed except as camouflage. All signs confirmed that her subterfuge was a success. Her quarry never appeared to suspect he was being followed even when she closed in on him once, considering and then rejecting the moment as the time for ambush.

By the time the trail led to frozen foods, Julia was feeling confident enough to eye him openly across the wide freezer that bisected the aisle. Just as she'd thought, he *was* absolutely perfect, with broad shoulders and slim hips, long, hard thighs and muscular arms that would spark more than a few ideas in any woman under the age of seventy. In sum, he was the stuff of which female fantasies were made.

Forget the fantasies, Julia told herself sternly. Fantasies, after all, were only supposed to be a means to an end—not their own objective. Idle daydreaming was nothing more than a waste of time, especially now when she was running short of that precious commodity. The only things standing between him and a clean getaway were the final stretch of the dairy aisle and the checkout. Soon he'd be lost to her forever, forcing her to enter him in the books as the one that got away. The one she *let* get away, she amended reproachfully as he rounded the corner for the dairy aisle and she hurried after him, resolving to run him to ground to prevent that from happening.

Finally, between the sour cream and cottage cheese, she ended the chase, abandoning her own buggy and stepping in front of his, bringing his progress to a sudden halt. When he made a move to steer around her, she caught the vinyl-coated wire edge of the cart. He tugged at his buggy, but she didn't yield, her fingers tightening even more firmly.

"Pardon me, ma'am," he said, making yet another futile attempt to go around her. While he had the physical advantage of greater strength, she had the powerful force of sheer determination—and desperation—in her favor. No matter how vigorously he tried to wrest the cart from her grasp, she refused to relinquish her hold. "Par...."

The words faded away when Julia raised her eyes and fixed them on his, her gaze wordlessly but decisively conveying that she had no intention of allowing anyone—even *him*—to thwart her successful attainment of her mission. The possibility that he wouldn't get the message never crossed her mind; she'd spent the last ten years perfecting her I-mean-business-and-no-mistake-about-it stare, and it never failed to achieve its intended purpose of establishing her authority.

His reaction was instantaneous, though not precisely what she expected. While he stopped pulling at the cart, he didn't let go; instead, his fingers tensed around the handle as inflexibly as hers gripped the front end. And when his eyes, brown with green and gold flecks, met hers, refusing to submit, he clearly couldn't restrain the spectrum of expressions, ranging from confusion to irritation to amusement to incredulity, washing across his face.

Julia was thrilled. Not only did he have great eyes that were a perfect complement to the rest of him, he had a wonderfully expressive face. Reining in her thrill at finding, through sheer dumb luck, a man with that invaluable quality, she asked, "How would you like to make a *lot* of money?"

He blinked, just once, before replying. "Define 'a lot.'"

He was even more perfect than she'd hoped. His accent was as pure Texas as longhorn cattle, bluebonnets and cowboy boots, which he was wearing. Who'd have thought she'd find an absolutely perfect man with a real Texas drawl in Quakertown, Pennsylvania, of all places? "A great deal. A substantial amount. *Very much.*"

The corners of his mouth twitched as if he were repressing the urge to smile and succeeding only by the slimmest of margins. Why he was bothering, she couldn't imagine. She'd give her right arm—and part of her left—to see him smile. "I know what the word means. What I wanted to know was what you consider a lot. To some people, ten dollars is a lot of money. To others, a million is only a drop in the bucket."

Matter-of-factly, she named an amount somewhere between the two and then waited silently for his reply.

"Who do I have to kill? Not that I intend to, mind you, but I have to admit I'm curious."

Julia gave him a shake of her head and a confident smile, positive he was as good as bagged. She could almost see herself, triumphantly bearing him back to her office in New York like a big-game hunter with a trophy. "No one."

He shifted uneasily from one foot to the other, and then asked, in a voice that clearly conveyed that he wasn't entirely certain he wanted to know, "So what would I have to do for this money, anyway?"

"I'm gonna make you a star."

To her astonishment, he began to laugh. Not a mere chuckle, either, but a full-fledged roar, as if she'd just told him the most hilarious joke he'd heard in months. She couldn't imagine what she'd said that was so funny, but, long after she'd expected him to collect himself, quit laughing and say something lucid, he was still howling so hard, tears glimmered in the corners of his eyes.

"Sir... Excuse me, sir, but...."

"A star!" he exclaimed, paying no heed to her effort to regain his attention. "A star!"

Julia sensed that he didn't believe her, though she was both serious and sincere. "I have my card right here...." She began digging in the bag slung over her shoulder, looking for the slim sterling-silver case in which she kept her business cards.

"A star! Lord, woman...." He went off again in a fresh new gale of laughter.

His response was so unsettling, Julia's hands shook as she hauled out the case, snapped it open, withdrew one of her cards and offered it to him.

Still laughing, he peered down at its embossed surface. The formerly uncontrollable laughter dwindled down to a mere chortle, intermittently punctuated by occasional sharp inhalations and a few lingering snorts. "Advertising?"

Assured that the subsidence of his mirth indicated his willingness to give her proposition the sober consideration it deserved, Julia nodded and began her pitch. "I'm working on the campaign to launch Ranger men's fragrances, and for the last six months..."

"Perfume?" His voice rose a full octave on the word, which was followed by a sputtering sound that seemed to augur renewed hilarity.

"After-shave and cologne, soap and deodorant, skin and facial-care products," she corrected him mechanically. While his reaction to the word *fragrances* wasn't a standard part of the spiel, her recital of the list of products was; they were supposed to come later in the program, though. "For the last six months . . ."

"Perfume?" he squawked again.

". . . we've been looking for a Ranger Man," Julia continued, undeterred, because she was at least marginally prepared for his laughter this time. "The people at Ranger were very specific about what they wanted for their campaign: masculine but not too threatening, rugged but not too raw, strong but not too burly, handsome but not too pretty.... In short, a man who epitomizes the idea of a Texas ranger."

"Perfume?"

"*You* are the very man we've been looking for."

He sighed deeply and shook his head. "I don't think so . . ." he glanced down at the card again before adding "Miss. . . ."

"Ms."

"Mzzz," he rectified, drawing out the word. "Adams. I'm not your Ranger Man."

"But you *are*," Julia protested. "Trust me. In the last six months, I've auditioned every male model and actor on the East Coast, and you're the closest thing I've seen yet. You even *look* like the artist's storyboards."

"But I'm not a model *or* an actor. I'm . . ."

"That's . . ."

". . . a dentist."

". . . all right. We can teach you," she assured him.

"*If* I were interested, which I'm not."

Julia paused, utterly dumbfounded by the claim. In her experience, everyone, male or female, young or old, beautiful or homely, secretly wanted to be a star. It was inconceivable that anyone would reject the prospect of fame and fortune without giving it so much as a second thought. He had to be kidding. Either that or he wanted more money. If he did, she could fix that; Ranger was prepared to be a lot more generous than their opening figure, which had been the amount she'd told him.

"Look, it's been real nice meeting y'all, Mzzz Adams, and I'm awfully flattered you think I could be this Ranger Man you're looking for, but . . ."

"Can you ride a horse?"

He didn't answer. Instead, he gaped at her, as speechless as she'd been moments earlier. What riding a horse had to do with anything was beyond him, and never mind the fact that he'd already refused her offer in no uncertain terms.

"It doesn't matter. We can use a double for everything but close-ups. How tall are you? Without the boots, I mean. Six-two? Six-three?"

Unless, of course, she was suffering from the delusion that he might change his mind if she badgered him long enough. "You aren't listening to a word I'm saying, are you?"

Tipping her head around the cart, Julia expertly gauged the height of the boots' heels and subtracted it before pronouncing, "Six-two."

"Of course you aren't. You're too busy playing Pygmalion. Look, Mzzz Adams . . ."

"Do you have hair on your chest?"

He couldn't have heard her correctly. She couldn't have said what he thought he'd heard. "Pardon?" Even as the word left his mouth, he knew he had heard her correctly, and she had said precisely what he thought he'd heard.

"Do you . . . Never mind, it's not important."

"Can y'all use a double for close-ups?" he asked. When the intended joke went ignored—and, apparently, ungotten—he sighed, shook his head and withdrew a plain, much-abused brown wallet from the back pocket of his jeans. After retrieving one of his own business cards, he handed it to her to show her what he'd already told her. "Read this. Please. See that 'DDS' after my name? It means I'm a dentist. You need a dentist, call me. You need a model, call a modeling agency."

Although she read the entire card, the only thing on it she really paid any attention to was his name. *Chance Palladin.* Good Lord, even his *name* was absolutely perfect. It conjured up images of cowboys and sagebrush and the Old West, when a man was a man, and a woman knew and appreciated it. "But I've already tried all the modeling agencies and . . ."

"You've been looking for the last six months," he completed for her, recalling what she'd told him no less than three times already. "I know, I know.... Look, I'm sorry, but . . ."

"Would you at least meet the client? Talk to him about it?" Her eyes begged him to reconsider.

"No." He shook his head firmly, telling himself that he was not going to be influenced by a pair of big brown eyes, no matter how plaintive they looked. "Positively not."

With a deep sigh, Julia finally relinquished her hold on the front of his cart. "You don't have a brother, do you?"

"Nope. Sorry. I'm one of a kind." Chance almost wished he could tell her he did; she deserved some sort of reward for her perseverance. Perseverance, hell; the woman was as tenacious as a hound with a bone.

"That's what I was afraid of." Julia stepped toward her own buggy, took its handle and turned back in the general direction of frozen foods. She had a lot of backtracking to do, not only to get rid of all this junk she'd acquired and pick up the things she'd actually intended to buy, but to find another Ranger Man—this time, one who wanted the job. Where she was going to find another absolutely perfect man, she didn't know. She guessed she'd have to check out every grocery store between New York and the Rio Grande.

"Mzzz Adams?"

"Yes?" She lifted her head and looked at him hopefully, wondering if maybe—just maybe—he'd changed his mind.

"Good luck. I hope y'all find your Ranger Man soon. And if you ever need a dentist . . ."

"Thanks," Julia answered automatically, so disconsolate, she hardly knew she spoke. All she knew was that she was no closer to finding a perfect man than she'd been an hour before.

As she retreated around the corner between dairy and frozen foods, Chance remained where he was, his eyes fixed on the center of her narrow back. He couldn't tear them away, any more than he could dismiss the encounter, finish his shopping, and be on his way. Her feet dragged and her shoulders sagged as though she'd just lost her last friend in the world . . . or, at the very least, her last hope of finding her Ranger Man. The last time he'd seen someone look that dejected, the man had just been told he needed two root canals, both of them with crowns, and the extraction of a wisdom tooth.

He felt the same odd pang of remorse he'd felt then, as if he'd been the source of the unhappiness, rather than merely the bearer of the bad news. He was sorry he couldn't help her, just as he'd been sorry he had to be the one to tell the man about the pathetic state of his teeth. He was not, however, the cause of Mzzz Julia Adams's trouble, any more than he'd been responsible for putting those lousy teeth in that man's mouth. He wasn't a model or an actor; he was a dentist, and he didn't have either the time or inclination to change his vocation.

Particularly *not* to become a model. A model for *perfume*, of all things.

God knew it was the last thing he'd expected her to suggest when she'd stepped in front of his cart. He'd thought she was trying to pick him up.

It had been a plausible assumption, if a bit presumptuous. He'd been aware of her following him since the meat counter. He'd noticed her watching his every move while she filled her cart with things that only made sense if she was paying less attention to their selection than to him, unless she was one of those crazy women with thirty-two cats and she actually wanted all those tubs of animal innards. Based on what he'd observed since his recent move from Houston, it could have been either case. For that matter, he still wasn't absolutely positive Miss—no, make that Mzzz—Julia Adams wasn't a crazy woman, with or without cats.

Who else but a crazy woman would pick him to be a male model for perfume? It was about as preposterous a notion as armadillos growing wings and taking flight.

Chance had to admit, however, at least to himself, it was a flattering offer. It wasn't every day someone told him he could be a star. For that matter, it wasn't every year. He simply wasn't flattered enough to say yes. It wasn't as if he were her last chance, after all. He was sure there must be dozens of men who'd be delighted to take her up on it. Hundreds. Thousands, maybe. Why hadn't she picked one of them? Him, a model for some men's perfume? Not hardly.

Especially not when he was a little disappointed that she hadn't been trying to pick him up. She was kind of attractive, in an uptight-serious-executive-female sort of way, with her hair all tied up in that thing on the back of her head and those big tortoise-shell glasses and blue jeans that looked as if they'd always been sent to the cleaners. He'd had the most inexplicable momentary urge to pull the pins out of her hair, whip off the glasses, and get those jeans wrinkled. It made him wonder if he'd been getting out enough since his move, a suspicion that was validated by the sudden impulse he had to go after her.

Doing his best to ignore it, he added a package of cheese and a loaf of bread to his basket and got in the checkout line. As he waited his turn, and waited again while his groceries were run across the scanner, bagged, and put back into his buggy, he let his mind drift, paying no attention to the beeps and clicks the cash register made as it tallied up his order. It was when the clerk read the total that he came back to earth with an abrupt thud.

"One forty-two, sixty-four."

Chance's head snapped up and he stared at the woman, uncomprehending. "Pardon?"

"That'll be $142.64, sir."

His head swiveled toward the cart and the four bags neatly tucked inside. There had to be some sort of mistake, he was sure of it. At least, he *thought* he was sure.

"Sir?"

And he'd figure out what the mistake was, just as soon as the cashier gave him the receipt, before he left the store and it was too late for them to fix it. In the meantime, he removed his wallet from his back pocket, took out all the cash in it and paid her. Clutching the battered leather, the meager folding portion of his change and the long strip of register tape, he wheeled the cart forward, next to the windows and out of the way, and stopped to look over the receipt.

There was no mistake. He'd bought every single item and, as far as he could tell, at exactly the price quoted. Disgusted, he folded the receipt, straightened the bills, and began to slide them into the long pocket in the wallet. As he did, they caught on the edge of the business card Mzzz Julia Adams had given him back in the dairy aisle.

Chance pulled it out and looked at it again. He wished she'd just been an attractive woman trying to meet him, instead of an advertising executive trying to hire him. He wished he'd had the presence of mind to ask her out, anyway, even after she'd told him what she wanted. And he wished he hadn't rejected her offer quite so adamantly.

God knew he could use the money.

His move from Houston to Pennsylvania had cost far more than he'd expected, as had everything else since his arrival. Housing and office rentals were higher than he'd anticipated, and so were salaries and medical coverage for his staff. When he'd ordered the equipment for his office, he'd been appalled to learn that he'd delayed doing so long enough to be the victim of yet another price increase. After he added in his own medical coverage, his malpractice insurance, and the payments on his college loans, his total expenses were astronomical. Under the circumstances, he wasn't sure he could afford to turn down *any* job that promised to pay real cash money.

And sounded so ridiculously easy. How hard could modeling be? He already knew how to ride a horse, and she'd said they'd teach him everything he needed to know, though what he'd actually need to know to stand in front of a camera and look "masculine but not too threatening" was beyond him. He suddenly hoped she'd meant it, however, as much as he hoped she hadn't been lucky enough to run into another potential Ranger Man during her second circuit of the store.

Apprehensive about the possibility, remote as it seemed, that she might be able to backtrack through the store, exchange the things she'd gotten for the things she actually wanted, pay for them and leave before his return, Chance rushed out to the parking lot, stashed his groceries in the cab of a pickup that was in roughly the same dilapidated condition as his wallet, and loped back to prop himself against the brick-face wall to wait for her.

He soon realized he'd overestimated the need to hurry. He could have taken his own sweet time with plenty to spare, because a full fifteen minutes elapsed between the time he returned and took up his post and the time she appeared in the checkout line. Another fifteen minutes after *that*, she finally pushed her buggy away from the register, across the stretch between the checkout and the windows and toward the door. She didn't look nearly as dispirited as the last time he'd seen her, but she still looked rather glum. Though it shamed him to admit it, her unhappy expression pleased him, because it meant she hadn't found someone else for the blasted job since then.

When she rolled her cart onto the rubber sensor mat, making the automatic door swing open, he levered himself away from the wall, drawing her attention. As soon as she caught sight of him, her expression changed as the gloominess dissipated and surprise and confusion and something that looked like wary optimism surfaced in its place. The sudden transformation made him smile, prompting another change, this time to something that looked positively hopeful. And, when he stepped in front of her cart, hooking his fingers over the front edge, her eyes lit up and the expression changed yet again into one of undiluted exultation.

They stood that way in the open doorway for several long moments, during which Chance made several observations that were as automatic as the mechanism of the door. Her buggy now held a fraction of its former contents, and everything he could see was fit for human consumption. Chicken gizzards and beef stomach had been replaced by a rump roast, frozen doggy treats by oranges and tomatoes. She wasn't a crazy woman—at any rate, not one with thirty-two cats; additionally, she was even more attractive than he'd reckoned earlier. Not merely attractive, but beautiful.

As far as he could tell, the difference in Mzzz Julia Adams's appearance—or, maybe, in his own perception of it—was the radiance supplied by her genuine elation. It made a staggering impression on him, knocking the wind right out of his lungs. It also irked the devil out of him that her reaction hadn't been generated by her delight at seeing him again, but by the fact that his presence suggested he'd changed his mind about becoming the Ranger Man.

The observations—and his consideration of the last one's thoroughly disconcerting implications—were interrupted by the sound of a throat being cleared, its source an elderly man who wanted to leave the store but couldn't because they were blocking the door. With a quick nod and an apology, Chance towed the cart the rest of the way out the door and over to one side, pushing it against the brick facade. Still holding the front of the basket, he fixed his eyes on hers and said, "I can ride a horse and I'm six-two and a quarter. Do you want hair or not?"

Her fingers clenched over the handle of the cart as she closed her eyes, turned her face heavenward and breathed, "Thank you, God."

"Hair?" he prompted impatiently.

"Some, but not too furry?"

He should have known; it sounded like all the other specifications she'd rattled off earlier. Precise, but not too exact. As far as he could determine without taking off his shirt and asking for her opinion, he wouldn't have to shave his chest, grow more hair, or be replaced by a double.

"How much did you say this job paid?"

As JULIA HEADED back toward her parents' house a short time later, every nerve in her body began to hum with the familiar excitement she always felt when things started to fall into place on one of her campaigns. It was a heady feeling, one she was sure she could never get enough of—and, God knew, if that were possible, she'd have found out about it by now, with ten years on Madison Avenue under her eelskin belt.

Instead, she liked it more and more every time. *Thrived* on it, in the most literal sense of the word. That anticipation—and the rush of adrenaline that went with it generated the energy she needed to market some of the most hopeless, and, in too many cases, ridiculous, products ever developed. Without it, she'd never have been able to provide the life support that had kept Sugar Tips, the world's first intentionally edible fingernails, on the market a full six months after they should have died a natural death.

Even though the patient had died, the operation itself had been a resounding success—as far as she was concerned. While she hadn't actually won any of the awards for which she'd been nominated as a result of that campaign, the fact that she'd been nominated meant the movers and shakers in the industry had noticed and liked her work. She could hardly wait until they got a look at Ranger, now that she'd finally found the perfect Ranger man she'd been searching for for six long months.

In fact, Julia could hardly wait until she got back to New York to share her excitement. While she loved her parents dearly and knew they loved her, too, they didn't understand her, her job or her ambitions. Even after all this time and all the evidence that it wasn't what she wanted, they still thought she ought to find herself a nice, safe job, settle down, and give them some grandchildren to spoil, the way everyone she'd known back in high school who still lived in Quakertown had done—or so she'd heard, since she hadn't kept in touch with any of them. There was no one left around here she'd want to share lunch with, let alone such wonderful news.

Which was why the phone company had made it so easy to reach out and touch someone these days, she reminded herself. Her parents had even given her a calling card so she wouldn't have to feel guilty about running up their bill and then having them refuse to let her pay for it. She didn't have to wait until she got back to New York to tell someone who'd actually be able to appreciate her accomplishment.

That someone, of course, was Denise, a tall, black woman who was her best friend and upstairs neighbor. She'd been a co-worker first, since she was working as a commercial artist for the same advertising agency... for now, at least, until she could support herself with her work as a *real* artist. Like Julia, she had big plans for her career. Plans that didn't include Locke, Reade and Hutchinson.

"Thank God!" Denise exclaimed once she got her on the phone and told her the good news. "I wasn't gonna mention it, but I was starting to worry you weren't gonna get this thing up and running before someone at Ranger realized the stuff actually smells like eau de swamp and they scrapped the whole project."

"Essence of road kill," Julia corrected her. "They'd be a lot better off if they could figure out how to bottle the *campaign* and sell it, instead. Or *him*, for that matter. It's amazing how much he looks like the guy in your storyboards."

"What's his name again?"

"Chance Palladin."

"For real?" There was a moment of silence, apparently while she considered it. "I like it. I'd give anything to meet the parents who gave it to him. It's got a certain ring to it, don't you think? 'Chance Palladin— Ranger Man.'"

"Sounds like a Western movie featuring Sam Elliott."

"Wesley Snipes, I think . . . but images like that are exactly why you like it too. Don't bother telling me you haven't entertained a few cowboy fantasies since you heard that name 'cause I won't believe it for a minute."

Julia didn't bother trying to deny it. Arguing with Denise was generally a waste of time and energy . . . especially when she was right.

"Now, don't you go forgetting all the little people who helped you get there when you've got your own agency. If I'm still drawing cockroach executions and cookie-loving cats by then, I wanna be doing it for you."

"You could always think about becoming my partner, and we'd both get out of there that much faster," Julia reminded her, as she did at least once a week. "We'd have the freedom to pick our own accounts and assistants, take the profits from our own work, get offices with our very own windows, in this century. . . ."

"And within six months, the NYPD would be investigating one of us for murdering the other. Like I told you when we discussed sharing an apartment, nothing screws up a friendship as fast as a fiscal relationship between two people with such different ideas about money. Besides, my game plan is to get out of advertising altogether, remember?"

"Right. There for a minute, I forgot."

"*Forgot*,' my ass. You were *choosing* to ignore it."

Once again, she was right. No hard feelings on either side.

"And, anyway. . . ." Denise assured her, ". . . you'll be able to do it by yourself, just as soon as you get the Ranger campaign up and on its feet."

As she hung up the phone, Julia hoped Denise was right about that, too. Getting the Ranger campaign up and running wouldn't be enough to do it on its own; she'd have to take Ranger and her other big accounts with her when she left.

Strictly speaking, hustling her accounts away from the agency wasn't ethical. She wasn't even sure if it was entirely legal. But in an agency that already had more partners than it knew what to do with, she couldn't see what other choice she had. *She'd* had the ideas and done the work and deserved more than the current crop of partners was willing to give, both in credit and compensation. She deserved to have it all and she was going to get it, in the next year, if everything went according to plan.

Finding Chance Palladin had put her back on track, pulling her out of the moody state she'd been in even before she'd left New York to come to her parents' house, leaving the file for the Ranger campaign on her dining room table. Now she wished she'd brought it with her, because this was the kind of energy that always enabled her to do a full month's work in a couple of days.

And her parents thought she should find herself a nice, safe job and settle down? Not if she could avoid it. She didn't have the slightest doubt that she'd wither up and die, like a plant in stagnant water, if she didn't have all the thrills and excitement that came from taking the chances that made the big difference on every one of her campaigns.

Which brought her back to Chance Palladin again. Talk about fate. He didn't know it yet, but the man was going to make her career.

2

THE FOLLOWING WEDNESDAY morning, back in New York, Julia wondered how much easier attaining her goals would be if she didn't have to contend with an assistant as useless as Rachel. She was sure it couldn't be any more trouble if she had no assistant at all; as it was, she had to do every last thing herself.

She'd made the coffee, which was freshly ground and brewed Kona, instead of the regular office sludge. She'd selected the Danish based on flavors and appearance, instead of sending Rachel to the bakery for "two dozen, mixed," the way she ordinarily did for meetings. And now, with Chance Palladin and the Fleischer brothers, who owned Ranger, all due in the office within the hour, Julia was setting the table in the conference room . . . while her so-called assistant watched her do all the work and prattled on about a seventies-style, disco-revival bar over in Brooklyn.

As she rearranged the pastries for the third time in as many minutes, Julia assured herself that all the fussing—bordering on fanaticism—wasn't excessive . . . or in any way connected with the prospect of seeing Chance Palladin again. If she was edgier than usual, that was only because so much was riding on the outcome of this meeting. If she'd spent an hour changing clothes before deciding on her favorite silk blouse (to relieve the severity of her tailored gray suit), her Joan & David suede pumps (to match the misty green of her blouse), and a dab from her seldom-used flacon of Joy perfume, that was only because little touches always made her feel more self-confident. If she'd been in the office that morning even before the night housekeeping staff had left for the day, that was only because she couldn't afford to overlook any detail, no matter how small.

Yeah. Sure. Right. And if she bought those flimsy excuses without so much as a flicker of doubt, she was probably game for buying historic bridges and a few acres of Florida swampland with resort potential, too, while she was at it.

Just admit it, already, and get it over with. You're a lot less excited about your fleshed-out plans for Ranger than you are about getting another look at the flesh you plan to employ for it—namely Chance Palladin.

Denise was right. Again. Chance Palladin wasn't just *every* woman's ultimate fantasy; he was *her* ultimate fantasy, too. Not that she was against fantasies on general principles. They were always fun—and could even be profitable, as Julia had learned in the ten years she'd been working in advertising. During that time, however, she'd also seen the truth behind the facade, and knew better than to believe that fantasies were anything more than illusions conjured up out of smoke and mirrors and a better-than-average imagination. More than most, she understood that losing sight of that fact—and control of the fantasies—was a sure route to trouble. Once that happened, they were bound to start interfering with real life and making a woman dissatisfied with what she actually had.

Real life, of course, was men whose hair was thinning just a little on the top, not quite enough to send them running to the pharmacy for hair tonic, but enough to make them be careful about how they combed it. Real life was just a hint of deskbound males' spreading rear that couldn't be disguised by artful tailoring or eliminated by too-occasional sessions at the gym. Real life was having to coordinate conflicting schedules and commitments until a date was nearly more effort than it was worth.

Real life was Barth Cameron.

In another, less enlightened era, Julia probably would have referred to Barth as her steady boyfriend. "Fiancé" sounded much too official, primarily because it *was*; they'd discussed marriage only in the most abstract of terms. "The man she was seeing" was a shade too casual to be accurate. And "lover" told the general public entirely more than she thought it needed to know about her private life. As Denise had often pointed out, it was no wonder people ended up using vague terms like "significant other" these days; nothing else seemed to fit.

She and Barth were partners in what could best be described as a comfortable relationship, one that had lasted for almost two years. They had a great many interests in common, including the theater, gourmet dining, and their careers. They had the same need for privacy on about the same timetable, so neither got on the other's nerves when he or she wanted to be alone. They read the Sunday *Times* in different, nicely compatible orders, so they didn't fight over who got what first—though there was the weekly tussle over who got to start the crossword puzzle and fill in the easy ones. And the physical side of their relationship . . . well, it wasn't bad, either, even if it didn't quite live up to the media hype. No earth shaking. No stars shattering. No skyrockets in the night.

If she'd allowed her expectations to be manipulated—and inflated—by a lot of overblown fantasies, she might have been *very* disappointed by reality. She knew enough, though, to keep both feet planted firmly on the ground and pointed in the right direction. She had to . . .

"Ohmigod. *Who* is *that?*"

Forcibly dragging herself back from her mental meandering, Julia followed Rachel's open-mouthed stare out the door to the reception area, where a tall man stood in the center of the room. He was wearing a suit that fit as if it were custom-made, but he didn't look entirely comfortable in it. His hair was perfectly trimmed and groomed, too, but he didn't look entirely comfortable with that, either. It wasn't until her eyes drifted down to the black cowboy boots—immaculate, but cowboy boots, all the same—that she realized who it was, and an uncontrollable chill shot through her. "Dear God, no!"

"Julia?" Rachel asked, her voice so breathy she might have been on the verge of fainting. "D'you know who that is?"

"That's Chance Palladin," Julia managed to choke out past the lump of shock and dismay wedged in her throat. This wasn't the same man she'd hired—or even the same species, for that matter. It was bad enough that he wasn't wearing jeans, but he'd gotten his hair cut—and, apparently, styled—since the last time she'd seen him.

Rachel's hand shot out to grip her elbow. "The Ranger Man? The guy you found for the campaign?"

"He was." Even through her dismay, Julia conceded that he was still fabulous-looking; he just didn't look the same. Instead, he looked like any one of the hundreds—no, *thousands*—of gorgeous male specimens she'd seen . . . tall, tawny and handsome, but appallingly tame.

"You found him in a *grocery store* in *Shakertown?*"

"Quakertown," Julia corrected her automatically as she headed toward the door. "In the produce section."

"I never found anything that looked like that in my grocery store," Rachel groused just as Chance caught sight of Julia and a broad welcoming smile took possession of his face. "Ohmigod."

Though she'd seen it before, Julia's reaction to that smile was every bit as strong as Rachel's. Unlike Rachel, she managed to restrain herself from being quite so blatant about it. It undoubtedly helped that she had other worries . . . foremost among which was that she might have time to fix this awful mess if she worked fast. After a glance at her watch told her just how fast she'd have to work, she grabbed Chance Palladin by the wrist and dragged him into the outer hall.

She was roughly half his size, and he could have resisted her if he'd made the slightest effort, but it never crossed Chance's mind to try. If Mzzz Julia Adams was so all-fired eager to be alone with him, he fully intended to accommodate her.

"What have you *done?*" she demanded.

Maybe being alone with him wasn't her top priority, after all. "Done?" Chance echoed blankly.

"The hair, the suit, the. . . ." she sputtered.

No *maybe* about it; being alone with him wasn't even in the running, as far as he could tell. "You didn't want me to gussy it up for the VIPs?"

"If I'd wanted a six-foot-two Connecticut Yankee in a blue pinstriped suit, I could've gotten one of those at any modeling agency in town. What I wanted was . . ."

"A man who's masculine but not too threatening..." he began, quoting the first part of her sales pitch from the week before. He forgot what came next, but, fortunately, she interrupted him before he proved he'd been laughing too hard to hear much of anything she'd said after that.

"What I wanted," she repeated, in slow, precise words, "was the image I saw last week. The one that fit the concept for the campaign."

Less appalled now, she surveyed him again, assessing him thoroughly. She probably studied corporate marketing projections in the same methodical way, he thought.

"I might be able to fix you if I work fast."

All right, maybe contingency plans, he amended. She plainly considered his current appearance a major disaster along the same lines as an oil or toxic-waste spill—and *she* was in charge of damage control.

"Please God, tell me you fit in clothes off the rack."

Though it sounded as if she was addressing the question to herself—or the Almighty—rather than to him, he immediately replied, "Y'all just tell me what you need, and I might be able to do better'n that."

Instead of giving him yet another of those point-by-point, specifically *un*specific answers, she tightened her lips in a perturbed frown; with no further warning, she reached up and raked her fingers through his hair, flipping her wrist in a way that tugged a lock of hair down over his brow. Though his entire sensory range suddenly narrowed down to his perception—and very sincere appreciation—of how cool, smooth and soft her fingertips felt as they brushed across his forehead, she seemed oblivious to the fact that he wasn't an inanimate object, but a flesh-and-blood man.

As if to underscore that impression, the expression on her face didn't change as, an instant later, with no warning at all, she stomped on his foot. It was definitely deliberate, too; he was sure of that even before she nailed the other one an instant later.

"You wanna tell me what you're doin' there?" Chance asked, bemused, though the what of it was self-evident; it was the *why* he didn't understand.

"Getting the right clothes isn't too much of a problem, but finding boots in New York in the time we've got to work with is another matter altogether—" she scuffed at his boots with her toe, as if she hadn't scratched the finish enough to suit her the first time around "—and those are way too shiny to've ever seen a horse, let alone been on one."

Well, of course they hadn't. What kind of idiot would have Charlie Dunn make him a pair of boots and then expose them to the natural byproducts of livestock? Custom-crafted boots were meant—and priced—to last a lifetime. Needless to say, these dated back to the old days, when he'd still had enough money to indulge himself that extravagantly.

"What kind of clothes d'y'all need?" he asked, seeing no point in trying to explain it to her; since moving north, he'd learned there were some things Yankees just couldn't understand, and the Texan passion for good boots was one of them.

"Like you were wearing last week—jeans and a work shirt, or maybe one of those Western ones with the snaps." Glancing at her watch, she added, "If we hurry, we oughta be able to get over to the Ralph Lauren department at Macy's and back by the time. . . ."

"Want me to go 'n' get 'em outta my pickup?"

Before the words were out of his mouth, Mzzz Julia Adams quit talking and smiled up at him. Beamed, actually. It was the same smile she'd given him the week before, when she'd found him waiting outside the grocery store: gloriously radiant, as if he'd done something utterly wonderful for—or *to*—her. It was so spectacularly dazzling, it made him wish he had.

"I'm not parked far away. Give me fifteen minutes—twenty, tops—and I'll be back."

JULIA DIDN'T KNOW how he did it, but Chance Palladin was as good as his word; seventeen-and-a-half minutes later—give or take a couple of seconds—he was back, clad in a faded chambray shirt and jeans and looking more like the same man she'd ambushed in the grocery store. Considering the way the soft, snug denim clung to the contours of his lower body, she couldn't imagine how he'd gotten his other pants off and into them—let alone dealt with the boots, too—so quickly.

Oh, yes, she could. Too well, as a matter of fact. In the process, she couldn't help forgetting to breathe—and, once she realized it, blushing like a schoolgirl who'd been caught peeking at the pictures in a dirty magazine.

Mercifully, the Fleischer brothers weren't witness to that spectacle, in all its unprofessional glory; they were stuck in the limo on the way from JFK. According to their last irritated call on the car's cellular phone, the latest in a series of bomb threats had all traffic coming into the city from the airport on the scenic route through Queens, and the best they could hope for at that point was to get there in time for lunch.

Which complicated her morning considerably; not only did she have to dispose of the Danish and find a caterer who was willing and able to do lunch on practically no notice, she also had to figure out what to do with Chance Palladin for the rest of the morning. Getting rid of the Danishes was easy, as simple as setting the tray in the coffee room and letting nature take its course. Getting hold of a caterer was going to be a tougher proposition, since Rachel, who—in theory, at least—should have been handling it, had taken it upon herself to handle Chance Palladin, instead.

"Could I get you some coffee?"

All right, so she really should have thought far enough ahead to send Rachel to her cubicle to work on lunch before he'd gotten back. As things stood now, if she didn't get her out of the vicinity—and soon—Julia was going to have to throttle her.

"Yes, ma'am, please . . . black," he answered, with a smile.

It looked as though Rachel intended to keep on making offers for as long as he kept accepting them— or until Julia stepped in and put a stop to it. Throttling Rachel looked like the only way to do it.

Now, now, she chided herself. Instead of being exasperated with Rachel, she ought to be thanking her for the endorsement—and thanking her lucky stars she'd found Chance Palladin. If every female in North America reacted the same way, Ranger was going to be the most successful product in history.

There was no reason to think they wouldn't, Julia silently added, once she'd managed to send Rachel back to work and hustled Chance Palladin into her office. Given the impact he had on her senses in wide-open spaces, she should have had some idea what the effect would be within the confines of her tiny, windowless office. Even retreating behind her desk didn't diminish

it; she was still close enough to see the enticing flecks
of color in his eyes, smell the woodsy scent of his cologne—which, thankfully, bore no resemblance to
Ranger—and feel the nearly irresistible impulse to find
out if his jeans were as soft, and the thighs beneath them
as hard, as they looked.

In an effort to keep both her thoughts and her gaze
off his thighs, Julia's eyes skated around the room,
seeking some other, less potentially embarrassing, tar-
get for her attention. Through a stroke of sheer luck,
one of the first things she spotted was the Ranger file
on her desk. If there was one topic that could distract
her enough to prevent her from making a complete fool
of herself in the next couple of hours, it was the campaign. Doing her best to forget about that "if," Julia
launched into her well-rehearsed spiel outlining her
plans for Ranger.

Within the first thirty seconds, Chance was sure he
was in way over his head, where both Mzzz Julia Adams and her campaign were concerned. He'd expected
to be out of his element when it came to the ads—what
did he know about advertising, after all, other than the
fact that it gave TV viewers a chance to answer the call
of nature or go to the kitchen for another cup of coffee
and piece of pie?—but feeling that way about *her*
caught him utterly by surprise.

While he certainly wasn't one of those good ol' boys
who still believed that women ought to be sweet young
things who never let a thought bother their pretty little
heads—a standard her assistant fit to a *T*—he'd never
found anything the least bit appealing about female
executive types who were so hellbent on clawing their
way to the top of their professions, they were only
marginally classifiable as female.

So then, why was he speculating that the fact that Mzzz Julia Adams wore sexy shoes and hundred-dollar-an-ounce perfume meant that, beneath her dress-for-success suits and no-nonsense demeanor, she also wore underwear that came in matching sets ... with lace?

"... There'll be a series of ten-, thirty- and sixty-second spots for TV and a matching set of color layouts for print," she was saying in a brisk boardroom manner that contrasted jarringly with the bedroom timbre of her voice. "We need to break right after the Fourth of July and get early exposure for the Christmas market, so we'll have to get moving. The deadline for August is only a month away...."

In the struggle to keep up with her breakneck pace, his idle—but very intriguing—consideration of her unmentionables had to be abandoned, but it was a wasted sacrifice. Speed was only part of the problem, since she wasn't speaking English, at least not any English *he'd* ever heard. At last, his head reeling with the effort of trying to make sense of it, he put up one hand to stop her like a traffic cop.

"... And, to get that Christmas feeling," she continued, not missing a beat, "we need snow for a few of the ads, so we have to do some location shooting up in northern Canada—probably just a day or two, which we'll schedule around your days off, the same as the rest of ..."

He tried again, refusing to allow himself to be defeated by one failed attempt. "Hang on a second. Stop. Please."

She did, though, if the puzzled expression on her face was anything to judge by, she didn't have a clue why he'd interrupted her. "Is there a problem?"

"Other than that I haven't understood a word you've said in the last ten minutes?"

She flushed bright pink, a sight he found encouraging—and endearing. Feminine, even, if he dared to call it that.

"Just for a minute, pretend I don't know any more about modeling and advertising and marketing than you do about fillings and root canals and gum disease."

Feminine, *definitely*. Chance decided he liked it when she got flustered and her cheeks turned the color of azaleas—and, if that made him a sexist, so be it.

But, sexist or not, his mama had raised a gentleman. He knew better than to embarrass a woman, and *this* woman was plainly about as embarrassed as it was possible for her to get. He automatically jumped to apologize, but she beat him to it . . . and with such remarkable grace, it bowled him over.

"I'm sorry," she said, smiling ruefully. "I said we'd teach you everything you need to know, and then, right off the bat, I make a liar out of myself, assuming you know things you wouldn't have any reason to know."

He returned the smile, pleased at the refreshing honesty she conveyed. "Can I let you know if you do it again?"

"Only if you promise you won't start telling me how to do my job once you understand the basics." She laughed, the sound low, musical and sexy. "If there's anything more irritating than a back-seat driver, I don't know what it is."

"Get a lot of 'em?"

She rolled her eyes. "Every model, photographer and makeup man I've ever worked with thinks they're an authority. Sometimes I think it'd be easier to work with animals, since they can't argue with me."

"Believe it or not, I get 'em, too. Picture a guy sitting in the chair with a suction tube in his mouth and a band around his second molar, his face numb from the Novocain, tellin' me how to put in a filling. Sometimes I just want to hand him the drill and tell him to go ahead and take a shot at it himself."

He'd wanted to make her laugh again, and he succeeded. It was just as tantalizing the second time around, even though there was something downright weird about her hair not budging an inch when she tossed her head. It was all anchored down again, this time in some sort of fancy braid that marched tightly over her crown and down to her nape. Did she think it would all make a run for it if she liberated it, or what?

Before Chance could reach a conclusion on that point—or reconcile himself to the fact that he was not going to pull out the pins just to see what would happen if Mzzz Julia Adams let down her hair—she started over, and he restrained himself in order to give her his undivided attention. This time she slowed down, made a conscious effort to use layman's terms whenever she could and explained unfamiliar words and ideas when she couldn't avoid them. Along the way, he learned that "break" had another meaning that didn't have a thing to do with either fine china or billiard balls.

All in all, the more Chance heard, the more at ease he felt with both his decision and the lingo . . . until he heard a word he was sure—or, more accurately, hopeful—he'd misunderstood.

"Billboards?" he echoed, wincing at the image. "You mean takin' a picture of me, blowin' it up so it's twenty feet across, and then slappin' it up on the side of the highway?"

"That's right," she confirmed.

"I don't think so." He frowned and shook his head. "I mean . . . I'm not sure I'm comfortable with the notion of becoming part of the landscape."

"Just think what it did for Tom Selleck," she offered.

"I'm not sure I'm comfortable with the notion of becoming the next Tom Selleck, either," he admitted. "But . . ."

"But nothing. Look, Mzzz Adams . . . I'm a dentist, not an actor or a model, and I'm just starting to establish a practice I can't afford to disrupt, no matter how much I can use the money." The assertion clearly bewildered her, prompting him to explain, "Yeah, I'm sure you thought somebody my age had been in practice for years, but I spent some time working in oil before I decided to go to dental school."

A lot of time, actually, but then the independent petroleum industry had bottomed out, making him reevaluate his career. After weighing his options, including a promising job offer from one of the big companies, he'd decided to go for safety and security, rather than risk any more time on something as unpredictable as oil. No matter what happened in energy policies, the economy or world politics, there would always be a need for dentists. No layoffs or terminations, so it was a safe, secure way to proceed to retirement age . . . assuming, of course, that he didn't go broke before the practice started to show a profit.

"I can't do anything about the billboards," she maintained. "They're part of the program, like the packaging and the name and the logo and the spritz ladies in the department stores and the personal appearances ..."

"Now, just stop right there," Chance broke in with a growl.

". . . and the . . ." she continued before finally winding down.

"Personal appearances?" he repeated unhappily. "I thought we were talking about only a few pictures and commercials, not all this other nonsense. I don't have the time to be takin' on another full-time job right now." He rose to his feet. "I'm sorry for the trouble, but I just can't do it."

"But . . ." Julia gaped up at him, panicking as she visualized the Ranger campaign and her career going up in simultaneous puffs of smoke. "We can . . . I can . . ."

"I'm sorry," the was-almost-the-Ranger-Man told her again. "It's just too much time, too much . . ."

"We can limit it to twelve appearances between now and Christmas," she said, coming to her own feet so she wouldn't have to look up at him so far—and so she'd be in a position to head him off if he made a run for it. "But the billboards have got to stay."

". . . exposure, too . . ."

"Ten. But the billboards . . ."

". . . much . . ." He turned and took a step toward the door, and she waffled between making an end run around the desk and vaulting over it. Over would probably be faster, but only if she didn't end up falling on her face on the way.

". . . have to stay. And eight appearances, at a thousand apiece."

"...too... Dollars?" He stopped short and spun back around to face her. "Extra? On top of what you told me last week?"

"That's right." As Julia nodded, a strand of hair escaped from her French braid and dangled against her cheek. Swiping it back into place, she noted that her skin was as hot as if she'd just finished a hard game of racquetball. "Please?"

For a moment, he continued to stare at her as if she'd just turned green instead of red, and then he took one tentative step toward the desk. "All right." After another step, he smiled and nodded, a bit more decisively. "I'll do it." At last, looking nearly convinced, he sat back down, settled into the chair, and retrieved his mug. "You've got yourself a deal."

Thank God.

"Eight appearances *and* the billboards?" she asked, checking to be sure they were clear and in agreement on the details. The last thing she wanted to do was to have to hash through this again in another couple of weeks.

He made a face before assuring her, "Eight, and the bill—"

A knock on the door interrupted him, and Julia called out for Rachel to enter, figuring she'd had enough time by then to set up lunch. She should have known it was too much to hope for, even before it turned out to be Barth, on his way back to his office from the coffee room, if the Danish he was carrying was any indicator. There was nothing unusual about him dropping into her office to chat, and usually she didn't mind. At the moment, however, she had too many other matters on her mind.

"So, the Ranger brass is still out on its tour of Queens and the Bronx, I take it?" Barth asked.

"Last I heard," she replied with a nod.

He shook his head sympathetically. "Damn terrorists. How's anyone supposed to get any business done in this city these days? They don't even need a bomb anymore, as long as they have a phone and know how to dial 911."

Julia knew he could go on at length on this subject; like a great many other New Yorkers, he resented the World Trade Center bombing not just for the death and destruction it had caused, but for the disruptive effect it continued to have on day-to-day life in the city. Even now, months afterward, the whole city all but shut down every time the authorities had to investigate another threat or abandoned package, just in case another one might turn out to be real. Wanting to avoid yet another tiresome tirade, she quickly intervened by introducing him to the man who had just agreed— again—to become the Ranger Man.

As the two men shook hands, Julia was immediately struck by the contrast between them. While they were roughly the same age, height and weight, Chance Palladin was leaner and harder and carried himself better. Disproving the adage that clothes make the man, he actually looked much more impressive in a pair of jeans and an ordinary chambray shirt than Barth did in an Armani suit. There was also an aura of relaxed masculinity about him, natural and earthy, devoid of the affectations and blustering that so many of her male colleagues substituted for genuine confidence. And, while she was at it, she could also note—just for the record—he had more hair.

"I guess you don't have to worry too much about terrorists down there in Dallas," Barth remarked, inexplicably making it sound as if it were a lack.

"Houston, actually," the other man corrected him. If Chance thought the comment was as odd as she did, he concealed his mystification with admirable skill. "At least until I moved up to Pennsylvania a few months back."

"To Quakertown," Barth said. She wasn't sure what his point was, exactly, but she *was* sure he had one; Barth rarely exerted himself, either physically or mentally, unless there was a point to it. "I've been there a couple of times. Quaint, but not much in the way of excitement, as far as I can tell."

The former Texan shrugged lazily, and she could have sworn his drawl was more pronounced than usual as he replied, "Enough to suit me, I reckon. These days, we've even got cable TV and pizza delivery, and Philly's just a ways down the road."

Suddenly recognizing the voice of John Wayne—and what was happening—Julia had to bite her bottom lip to keep a straight face. Barth was all but calling him a hick from the sticks, trying to draw him into some testosterone-inspired one-upmanship game, and Chance Palladin was refusing to play. Barth didn't seem to know what to make of it; most men he knew were as eager as he was to compare their respective salaries and perks, the square-footage of their co-ops, and the views from their office windows. He hadn't been amused when she'd once pointed out to him that it was simply the grown-up version of "mine's-bigger-than-yours."

"But it certainly isn't like living in the Big Apple," Barth countered.

Chance tightened his mouth, suppressing an amused smile. It was all too apparent to him that Barth was a blowhard, so full of hot air and himself, he was constantly looking for new venting outlets. As strong as the urge was to poke a pin in him and end that need, he checked it, sensing that Mzzz Julia Adams and her bosses might not look too kindly on it if he permanently deflated her colleague.

"I guess not," he mildly agreed, and then watched Barth turn an interesting shade of fuchsia, clearly frustrated.

"You'll find some of the finest restaurants in the world in New York, the best museums, the theater... Julia, that's why I stopped in in the first place," Barth said, interrupting himself, losing interest in Chance, and returning his attention to her. "Ted Bell's got a pair of tickets he doesn't need for that new Andrew Lloyd Webber, and he called to see if we want them."

"'Tickets he doesn't need'? For the new Andrew Lloyd Webber musical?" Julia's voice rose in disbelief, and then comprehension hit an instant later. "Did you win them playing squash or are he and Vanessa on the outs again?"

"She broke it off last Friday. Again. Something about the premarital contract, I think."

Lacking interest in the premarital woes of Ted and Vanessa, Chance mentally backtracked to the part where Barth had said "if we want them." *We,* as in the two of them being a couple? Mzzz Julia Adams and this jerk? He'd heard things were getting tough for women in the big cities these days, but there was a world of difference between tough and downright ridiculous.

Stranger things had happened, though. Lots of stranger things. He'd agreed to become the Ranger Man, for one.

Chance watched as she thumbed through her appointment book, checked the date Barth cited, and reached for a pencil.

"*Ink*, Julia, *ink*," Barth muttered with a frown. "Do you have any idea how hard these tickets are to get? If you're not sure, I know someone who'd cough up a hundred apiece for them—but he's not gonna want them at the last minute."

So, all those gray smudges in her appointment book weren't just a reflection of how frequently Mzzz Julia Adams's demanding schedule forced her to reschedule or cancel business engagements. Judging by Barth's insistence on "ink," she made a habit of rescheduling and canceling *him*, too—regularly enough that he now anticipated it.

Though she obediently swapped the pencil for a pen—this time—Chance was still savoring that thought when Rachel came careering into the room without knocking, looking as harried as if she'd given up looking for a caterer and made lunch herself.

"I did it, Julia! The caterer'll deliver lunch for five at noon, you've got the conference room until two-thirty and Abdul just called to say they were crossing the Queensboro Bridge."

"They'll be here soon," her boss answered, rising from her seat and smoothing her skirt as Rachel darted back out into the hall, presumably to broadcast her accomplishment to the rest of the office. "I'll see you tonight, then, Barth . . . you *are* still coming for dinner?"

"Damn, I meant to tell you about that, too. I've got to reschedule. The marketing team from Starways decided to fly up a day early, so I've got to take them out tonight and show them a good time."

"Starways Airlines?" Chance asked, despite his very limited interest in the subject. He found the discovery that the rescheduling and canceling were mutual a far more fascinating topic. "I thought they went belly-up."

"They're seriously listing to one side, but not dead yet," Barth corrected him. "I'm working on a campaign that's guaranteed to get them back on an up-swing."

So, Barth wasn't just a jerk; he was an idiot, too, if he believed what he was saying. Even *he'd* heard the reports that Starways's bankruptcy was just a matter of filling out the paperwork.

"Well, good luck," he offered doubtfully.

"Thanks," Barth replied, apparently oblivious to the lack of sincerity. "I'll give you a call when I get in, Julia. Knowing those guys, I don't think it'll be very late."

As she nodded, she didn't look particularly thrilled at the prospect, but Barth didn't appear to notice that, either. Unless Chance was mistaken—and he didn't think he was—the man had no idea she didn't think he was the greatest thing since sliced white bread. That conviction said a lot more about his ego than it did about her acting abilities. It was also conclusive proof that he was, bar none, the biggest blowhard, jerk and idiot Chance had ever met in his life.

Surely Mzzz Julia Adams could do better than that.

3

CHANCE HAD A LOT OF TIME to think about that issue—three hours, to be precise. If it felt more like three *years*, that was because it had taken the Fleischer brothers, Ranger's owners, no more than five minutes, tops, to give him a good look-over and approve him. Why they hadn't let him go at that point, he wasn't sure. Their discussion with Mzzz Julia Adams might as well have been in Urdu for all of it he'd understood. Now that it was finally over, the only thing on his mind was how soon he'd be able to muster up enough energy to climb into his pickup and head for home.

"Would it help if I told you that you shouldn't have to come to any more of these meetings?" she asked, propping her bottom on the edge of the conference-room table between his long-cold mug of coffee and an orderly stack of multicolored index cards.

"That all depends..." he began, studying the way her skirt pulled tautly across her hips and thighs. It was a distraction nearly effective enough to convince him to accept the first good news he'd heard all day at face value. He'd been around enough, however, to know that any offer that sounded that good had to be too good to be true. "Can I consider that a promise?"

"Probably."

"Probably not, then," he assured her, unhappily recognizing that he'd been right.

"*Highly* probably?" she amended, sounding as if she hoped the slight difference would be enough to settle the issue.

It wasn't. Honesty was fine, but it would have made him a lot happier if she'd simply told him what he wanted to hear and crossed her fingers behind her back while she did it. He wouldn't have believed her, but it would have let him drop the subject until he was in a better frame of mind to deal with it. At the moment, the memory of this meeting was still entirely too fresh in his mind. "How highly?"

"Almost definitely," she tried again. "With the amount of money Ranger's paying a dozen different teams of consulting, marketing, and advertising experts to keep them working on a project that's already as far over budget and behind schedule as NASA's plans to build the space station, I wouldn't think they'd be interested in spending more time and money shuttling back and forth between Chicago and New York and holding meetings just so they can have a nice lunch and watch the model doodle."

Chance flushed hotly. In his defense, he hadn't been doodling; he'd been making a list of how the money he'd be getting from this job had already been spent and trying to figure out whether or not there'd be anything left for him to do something fun with once the bills were paid. He opened his mouth to tell her that, closed it, and then tried again, but the only sound he managed to force out was a choked "I . . ."

"Gotcha."

She grinned impishly, and he returned it, though less enthusiastically. Not because she'd gotten the best of him, but because he couldn't begin to match the level of excitement that had energized her all afternoon.

While he felt as if he'd been run over by a truck, she looked as if she was ready to go out and run a couple— or a couple *dozen*—brisk laps around Central Park. "So, besides being bored enough to retreat into the ozone, what'd you think?"

Think? About what? He was still struggling to figure that out when she went on, still at lightning speed.

"It went really well, didn't it? They absolutely loved you, and the idea of two different themes—one macho, like the Marlboro or Nike ads, and the other sensitive and sexy, like Chanel or Calvin Klein—seemed to go over just the way I hoped it would. It's been done before, naturally—but, by now, there isn't much that hasn't. . . ."

Not excited, Chance suddenly realized. *Wired*. She was so pumped with adrenaline, she was positively glowing with it: all pink-cheeked and dewy-eyed and dazzlingly, indisputably, female.

It's probably the same way she looks after great sex. With Barth? Not hardly.

The two thoughts came in such rapid succession, they were practically simultaneous, and trying to convince himself that he didn't know where either one had come from would be a pure waste of energy he couldn't afford to spare right now. It was no coincidence that he'd been overwhelmed and confused from the moment he'd stepped into the agency's office, but he'd only been bored and irritable since Barth's arrival on the scene.

"...so now I've got these lobsters in a paper bag, and if I don't cook them tonight, they'll die."

A moment of silence passed before it occurred to Chance that she was waiting for an answer. Unfortunately, he'd been caught up in his thoughts about Mzzz

Julia Adams and Barth and great sex—though connecting the middle one with either of the other two took
the kind of imagination he just, thank God, didn't pos-
sess—so he had no idea what the question had been.

"Pardon?"

"Lobsters," she repeated. "Two of them, in a grocery bag in my refrigerator, with a maximum life ex-
pectancy of another twelve hours. Whether they die in
vain or give their all for a glorious cause is entirely up
to you."

"You're inviting me to dinner?"

"If you'd like." Chance smiled, so pleased and surprised that he forgot how exhausted and eager to get out
of the city he'd been just moments earlier. It wasn't *that*
far to Quakertown, he reminded himself; he could stay
another couple hours and still get home at a decent
hour. And, if the point that they'd been Barth's lobsters first and he hadn't had enough sense to stick
around for them made him want to gloat a little at his
loss, well . . .

"I'd like."

JULIA LIKED, TOO. Though the invitation to dinner had
been as much of a surprise to her as it had clearly been
to him—her initial solution to the lobster surplus had
been to see if Denise was interested in a free dinner—
she couldn't say she regretted the impulse. It couldn't
hurt for her to get to know the man a little better, now
that he'd agreed to play the instrumental role in fulfilling her career dreams. Besides, he deserved more than
even a lobster dinner for being such a good sport.

He'd been a good sport all day—through the un-
scheduled change of clothing and Rachel's fawning, the
hours of waiting and Barth's goading, the long meet-

ing and then still more waiting while she got ready to leave the office—even though she knew he must have been bored beyond endurance. She was sure she'd feel the same way—and probably not behave nearly as well—if she were forced to sit through a seminar on gum disease.

Being a good sport didn't mean he'd been agreeable to the point of tractability. He hadn't hesitated to challenge her on the questions of billboards, personal appearances, and his attendance at future meetings. If, when all was said and done, she'd had her way on all those issues, that was only because, in each case, her way had been right.

Their most recent skirmish had been on the sidewalk in front of her office building as they'd been leaving. It had started to drizzle, making it cold and damp and ugly in a way unique to New York at the end of February, so she'd suggested they get a cab—Ranger's treat—rather than taking the subway downtown to her apartment in Greenwich Village.

"But, my pickup . . ." he'd protested, trying to steer her in the general direction of a nearby parking garage.

"Your pickup? You drove into the city?" She'd stopped and stared at him, so incredulous, she'd barely noticed the chill or the wind. She'd vaguely recalled hearing him mention it before, but, at the time, she'd been a lot more concerned about getting him into different clothes than about where he'd be getting them. "What on earth possessed you to do *that?*"

"I thought it'd be like driving in Houston. Guess what? I was wrong."

"I'd say so." She'd wanted to point out that driving in a demolition derby would have been a closer comparison.

"Trust me. It's a mistake I won't make a second time. But, since it's here. . . ."

She'd started shaking her head the moment she realized what he'd been suggesting. It had been a bad idea...a very bad one. "If it's here, it should stay here."

"But, don't you think . . ."

"I don't think—I *know* you should leave it where it is for now, and then take a cab back later to get it."

"But . . ."

"If you try to take that truck into my neighborhood, you're gonna find out the hard way why buying a car never even occurred to me."

By the time their cab had reached her apartment in the Village, he'd been ready to concede that she'd been right. In Greenwich Village, parking a car was an even tougher proposition than driving one. He'd taken one look at the row of bumper-to-bumper cars that lined her narrow street—a typical state in the Village—and shuddered like a man who'd just escaped a fate worse than death. "The pickup's got a clutch and no power steering. Even if we'd found a space, it would've taken me an hour to get into it."

"And the last time there was a vacant space on this block, Jimmy Carter was in the White House."

It had been considerably longer than that since there'd been a vacant apartment, at least officially, due to that peculiar New York institution known as rent control. As rents had skyrocketed throughout the rest of the city, a relative handful of buildings had had their rents frozen years before, allowing their landlords only occasional—and minimal—rent increases. With the rents on the apartments in this block now at less than a quarter of the rates being asked for similar non-rent-controlled apartments, the rare openings tended to be filled by the other tenants' friends, who learned about them by word of mouth. Julia was no exception; she'd heard about her apartment from Denise.

Denise had also been her guide as she'd made the transition to living in the Village, teaching her where to shop, when to put out her garbage without getting a ticket from the sanitation police . . . and how to ignore things like the harsh scraping noise that marked the departure of their cab, along with a substantial strip of paint off a parked Chevy Malibu old enough to vote.

"Third time this month that car's been hit," she'd remarked matter-of-factly, before he could get any ideas about getting the cab's number, tracking down the Chevy's owner, and reporting it.

He'd shaken his head, plainly bemused, and then followed as she'd negotiated the tight space between the bumpers of two other cars—both of which had rust, dents and No Radio signs in the windows—to get to the curb. "Thanks for making me leave my pickup in the garage. It isn't much, but I'd kind of like to keep what's left of it awhile longer."

"Are you gonna get all huffy if I tell you I told you so?"

"Will it stop you if I say yes?"

"Probably not."

"I won't bother, then. . . ." he'd assured her as she'd unlocked the row of deadbolts that guarded her door and opened it. *"Wow."* He'd dragged the word out as he'd stepped into the apartment and looked around in obvious admiration.

Julia appreciated the advantages to renting an apartment at sixties' rates in the nineties, especially having extra money to spend any way she liked. Shortly after she'd moved in three years earlier, she'd reasoned that fixing up her apartment made a lot more sense there than it had in her old, much-higher-priced place. She'd spared no expense in doing it, but it had been worth every penny. How else would she have had a working fireplace to curl up in front of with lobsters, melted butter, and Chance Palladin?

Now, there was an image to make a woman's mouth water. Not just any woman's, but *hers*. She'd only claimed to be reasonable about fantasy, not immune to it.

"This place looks like a feature in *Metropolitan Home*," he remarked, his eyes sweeping from the Bukhara rug to the Lalique goldfish on the burled maple cocktail table to the hand-painted *faux* marble mantle as if trying to absorb it all at once. "Does that fireplace really work or is it just for show?"

After the lurid thoughts she'd been entertaining about that very fireplace, Julia wasn't surprised to feel her face go hot. God willing, it wouldn't show in her voice, too. "It not only works, it has a gas jet to start it. Just throw on some logs and push the button, if you want, while I get out of my work clothes."

While she was gone, Chance set the logs and lit a fire. It worked just as easily as she'd claimed, with none of the tinder, kindling and cursing that made a fire in his own fireplace back in Quakertown nearly more effort than it was worth. By the time she went through to the kitchen and returned with two glasses of white wine, he was already sitting on the couch and enjoying it.

"I *want* one of those," he said, still staring into the fire.

"A fireplace?" She sat beside him, close enough so the soft fabric of her top brushed against his bare forearm as she leaned forward to set the glasses on the table next to a colorful school of glass fish.

"A push-button fire," he clarified, turning to look at her. She had on an outfit that looked like sweats, but was made out of a stretchy velvet that clung to curves her dress-for-success suit had done its best to deny. She looked soft and feminine—and so touchable, he could hardly resist the urge to do just that. Somehow managing to retain the thread of their conversation in spite of that, he asked, "Are they expensive?"

"The gas jet?" She nibbled her lip as she thought about it, and then shrugged. "To be honest with you, I don't remember."

He'd been like that once, too...back in the oil-boom days, when money had been easy to come by, and just as easily gone. He reached for the glass of wine, reminding himself that dwelling on the past was just being maudlin sometimes, not nostalgic. "I can only have one glass, you know. I'm driving home, and it's pretty far." He took a sip, intending to make it last. "Know anything about bus service from Quakertown?"

She smiled like a woman who'd just been proven right. "I know *everything* about bus service from Quakertown . . . or, at any rate, I've got all the information in my files. I'll have Rachel send you a copy first thing in the morning."

"You sure you trust her with it?" Chance asked doubtfully, trying not to return her smile. It had been a day with lots of giving-in—all his—and he didn't want to encourage her into thinking she'd established a pattern.

She groaned. "It was that obvious?"

"Julia, how in the hell'd you get saddled with an assistant that's so utterly useless she can barely order lunch?" He used her name without the Mzzz for the first time and it felt right to do so—though he couldn't quite figure out why.

"*Where* in the hell is more like it," she muttered under her breath.

"And, more importantly, why in the hell d'you keep her?"

"Her mother was a Rivers—of Rivers Textiles, one of our biggest accounts—and they all thought an ad agency would be a good place for Rachel to meet eligible men." She smiled sweetly—too sweetly to be believable—before adding, "And I lost the lottery and had to take her for her first six-month stint."

Chance allowed the smile to turn into a chuckle, though he was sure that being stuck with Rachel wasn't at all funny, as far as Julia was concerned. "How much longer before you get to hand her over to the next unlucky contestant?"

"A hundred and two days."

It didn't surprise him that she could tell him precisely how many days she had left; if he were in her shoes, he'd be counting hours, too. "No chance of time off for good behavior?"

"Only if she snags some eligible man, marries him and moves to Scarsdale," she grumbled, rising to her feet. "I'd better go check on the water. It should be getting hot enough."

As she set off for the kitchen, he got up and followed her, bringing their glasses with him. "Any prospects yet?"

"Prospects?" she echoed blankly.

"For Rachel," Chance reminded her, looking around the room. If advertising ever went the way of the independent oil industry and the dodo, she could run a catering service out of there. She already had everything she'd need, from a big restaurant stove to every kind of cookware he'd ever seen to utensils and appliances he'd never seen and couldn't identify. From the looks of it, she took her cooking mighty seriously.

"You interested?" Julia asked in a voice that sounded oddly strained, digging through the refrigerator until she came up with a covered plastic dish, butter, a lemon, and the brown paper bag.

"In Rachel?" He took the bag and set it in the sink. "Do I seem like the kind of man who'd be interested in a bubbleheaded idiot like her?"

When she didn't answer, Chance realized he'd inadvertently insulted her and wondered if she realized it, too. Did *she* seem like the kind of woman who'd be interested in a bigheaded idiot like Barth? He floundered around for a graceful way of redeeming himself, but everything he thought of seemed sure to make matters worse. If he'd just watched what he'd said in the first place...

"The only kind of man who'd be interested in Rachel...." she finally said, her thoughtful tone demonstrating that she'd merely been considering the question, and not its implications, "...for any length of time, at least, would be someone who didn't want a woman as much as he wanted a pretty pet."

"Exactly," he agreed, simultaneously breathing a sigh of relief and reflecting that, according to that description, Barth and Rachel were ideally suited for each other. "And, as far as I'm concerned, a cocker spaniel would be cheaper, smarter, and a damned sight less irritating. At least, it couldn't talk."

Before Julia could reply, there was a knock at the door, and she set down the knife and wiped her hands on a tea towel. As she headed into the living room to answer the summons, Chance prayed that Starways hadn't filed for bankruptcy that afternoon, leaving Barth free to come to dinner, after all.

A moment later, even that thought fled his mind in the pure confusion generated by her parting request. "If you could start the salamander while I'm gone, it'd be a big help."

Salamander?

He had to have heard her wrong. He was sure of it. She couldn't have said "salamander"—could she?

What the hell would she use it for? Sauce?

Though his mind maintained—quite reasonably, he thought—that Julia didn't really intend to cook a newt, which no one in their right mind would want to eat, even if they were edible, and he was fairly sure they weren't, he cautiously unfolded the top of the bag and peered inside. Nothing black, slimy, and ugly as sin in there . . . only a couple of magnificent specimens of the Pride of Maine. Tipping the sack, he gently dumped them into the sink, where they wriggled listlessly, blowing bubbles and flexing their claws against the fat rubber bands that held them shut.

No newt is good newt, he assured himself, seeing that the lobsters didn't have a friend. Absurdly, he imagined that the cold, dark confines of the refrigerated bag had alerted them to their death-row status, and they'd decided a plump, juicy salamander would be a perfect main course for their last meal. He was still staring down at the lobsters, still grimacing at the thought, when Julia came back into the room.

"Don't you dare go naming those things unless you've already called out for Chinese delivery," she warned him. "I was having enough trouble with Rachel even before the terrorists shut down every direct, above-ground route between JFK and Manhattan, so I was too worked up to eat lunch once it finally got there, and . . ."

"What, exactly, *is* a salamander?"

Considering that he'd spent the entire day contending with an endless series of unfamiliar words and unfamiliar meanings for words he'd always thought he understood, he probably should have realized that "salamander" wasn't going to buck the trend. He probably would have, too, if he hadn't been pondering—and dreading—the grisly possibility that Barth was at the door.

Which he hadn't been, it seemed, unless she'd told him he'd missed his opportunity and sent him on his way without his supper. It was good news, either way.

"A salamander," she replied, in the same patient manner in which she'd explained all those complicated advertising concepts, "is part of the range."

He'd guessed she didn't mean like "Home on the . . ." either, even before she went to the stove, pointed out an open box at its top, and turned a knob and pushed a button beside it. In instant response, flames whooshed downward inside it.

Leaning down a bit to peer in once the flames had subsided to a less threatening level, Chance bluntly observed, "So, it's a broiler."

"Not exactly," Julia corrected him.

"And how not, exactly?" he asked, straightening to his full height and crossing his arms over his chest.

It was an impressive height, too...nearly as impressive as his chest, which was conveniently situated at eye-level now that she wasn't wearing shoes. Pulling herself up to *her* full height—merely six inches less than his without the boots; though, at the moment, the difference seemed like more—Julia asserted, "It's got adjustable levels so it can melt food slowly enough not to brown it *or* brown it fast enough not to dry it out...."

With a twist of her wrist, she lowered the flame until it barely glimmered in the dark box; an instant later, she turned it up to a level she'd seen turn a slice of bread into charcoal dust in a matter of seconds. Leaving it there, she went on, "And it's got vents to draw out the steam so the food doesn't get soggy...."

More frustrated by his look of tolerant amusement than by her limitations at demonstrating the salamander's features, Julia chopped the butter in half, slapped the chunks into the warmers' ramekins and then transferred potatoes to an aluminum au gratin pan with enough force to flatten their bottoms and make them sit up straight. "And it's..."

"...a broiler," he said again equably, reaching to turn the heat down to a more moderate setting and sliding the potatoes in on its roll-out rack. "What d'y'all got against plain English, anyway? Is it against your religion, or just company policy?"

"I'm getting a lecture on plain English from a man who can use the words *y'all* and *reckon* in the same sentence and still keep a straight face?"

"At least I don't use *impact* as a verb."

"Oh?" Julia challenged, knowing she had him cornered. He'd walked right into it, too, she told herself gleefully. "And what do wisdom teeth do?"

"Bad example," he conceded. "And I had so many other really good targets to pick from, too . . . like the business about how ads are *supposed* to break, or . . ."

She glared at him, lips pursed in exasperation. While it might sound as if he were chiding himself for the oversight, the look in his eyes told another story.

"Gotcha."

He grinned unrepentently. He was entitled. She'd thought she had him only because he'd wanted her to think so—when, in fact, *he'd* had *her*, instead. She could have resented it, if she hadn't found that particular variety of playful audacity so oddly appealing. Devastating, even.

Devastating? Why does Denise have to be right all the time?

Just minutes before, when Denise had stopped in on her way home from work, established that the rumor that Chance Palladin was at Julia's for dinner was more than just water-cooler gossip, and raised her eyebrows in that way that said volumes without her uttering a single word, Julia had staunchly denied that she had any designs on the Ranger Man that weren't strictly professional. Denise, being Denise, had immediately asked which one of them she was trying to convince.

Either way, it hadn't worked. Denise had been smirking by the time she'd left, and Julia had been able to feel her ability—and, for that matter, her *will*—to suppress her decidedly unprofessional response to him deteriorating by the second ever since. At the rate it was going, she didn't know how much longer she'd be able to keep herself from sticking the lobsters back in the refrigerator, dragging him into the living room, and seeing what she could do about having her wicked way with him in front of the fire. Unless she was mistaken—and she didn't think she was—he'd take to that idea with considerably more enthusiasm than he'd been able to muster up for either personal appearances or billboards.

Talk about a fantasy.... Julia felt a lot warmer than could be accounted for by the steam from the pot of boiling water, and she couldn't help wondering if it were actually possible for the steam generated by the fantasy to heat up the room.

"Julia?" Chance breathed, as the latest in the succession of expressions that had captured her face since the glare had faded rendered him nearly speechless. It was hunger, plain and simple, and the kind that had nothing to do with the fact that she hadn't eaten lunch. She might have treated him as though she thought he was a display object that morning, but he had no doubt that she was now very much aware he was a man. Even the steamed-up lenses of her glasses weren't enough to obscure the expression in her eyes—so blatantly sexual, he wondered how he ever could have thought of her as only marginally female.

Why, Julia, I never would have guessed you had it in you....

But he had. Why else would he have become all but obsessed with whether or not she wore matching underwear with lace, and how she'd look—and *act*—if she let her hair down?

As if he'd brought it about just by wanting it so badly—though he knew the steam had a lot more to do with it than his wishes did—several dark strands pulled free from her braid to straggle around her face. Lifting his hand, he touched one loose wisp at her temple, and it coiled around his finger, soft and slightly damp, as if it were animate. Staring at it, he couldn't help conjuring up a whole series of creative, provocative scenarios in which various parts of her body were wrapped around his even more intimately than that curl. He moved his hand, stroking his knuckle and the silky hair down her cheek, and was gratified when he heard her suck in her breath sharply, and then release it in a long, slow purr.

"So beautiful," he whispered, meaning not just her features, but her naked desire. He'd always thought there was nothing more powerfully arousing than a woman who wanted him enough to show it with such plain honesty. And she did. As he shifted his fingers down to cup the curve of her jaw and hooked his thumb beneath her chin, he didn't have to draw her closer to him and turn her face up to his. She did both of those things entirely on her own, and because she *wanted* to do them. "So sweet...."

This last bit of praise was a sigh that went directly from his mouth into hers, already open in ardent demand. He wasn't sure which of them had initiated the kiss, and, at the moment, he didn't much care.

He doubted he ever would. All that mattered was that her mouth was soft, warm and moist, fitting his as perfectly as if they'd been designed as a matching pair. He was positive their bodies would fit together just as perfectly... that is, when he wasn't wearing boots or she wasn't in her stocking feet. As it was, he was a little too tall—or she was a little too short—for the complementary curves and hollows of their bodies to correspond the way they should. She had to stand on her toes to nestle her breasts in the shallow ledge beneath his chest, and when he cupped his hands under the round swell of her bottom to help hold her there, it occupied them both, preventing him from touching anything else.

At last, frustrated, Chance slid his hands to Julia's waist and boosted her up to sit on the countertop. If it made *her* a little higher now, the fact that it also freed up his hands and enabled him to step in tight between her legs more than made up for it. Extolling both of those benefits, he took off her glasses with one hand and placed the other on her knee where it rode the waistband of his jeans. He couldn't say what he did with her glasses after that. Most of his attention was with his other hand as it roved up the velvet-covered length of her thigh and slid under the loose hem of her top as it approached her hip.

As her lips escalated their demands on his, Julia whimpered pleadingly and fidgeted on the cool, hard surface of the granite-topped counter. Hooking her calves around his waist, she pulled him in even closer, the sudden motion dislodging his hand so it glided up to the bare skin at her waist. For a moment, she held her breath as his fingertips, slightly rough, strummed aimlessly against her flesh; she let it out only once they settled into a deliberately seductive rhythm that made every cell in her body hum in response. Her breasts tightened in anticipation of his touch, her heart beat more quickly, and her most feminine places ached . . . why, even her *toes* curled against the small of his back.

Threading her fingers through his hair, she kissed him more eagerly, not just on his mouth, but on the high arches of his cheeks, on his brow and even on his closed eyelids. When he traced the tip of one finger along the lace trim of her bra, down one cup into her cleavage and up the other side to her strap, she shivered despite the room's warmth, and then repaid the favor by gently biting the rim of his ear and soothing it with her tongue.

"Julia...."

Feeling his body twitch in reaction as he moaned her name, she tried to do it again, but his ear wasn't there anymore, only the top of his head. Before she could collect herself enough to puzzle about the switch, the reason for it became apparent as she felt his mouth touch her chest between her collarbone and the top of her bra.

It was a struggle to open her eyes—and she couldn't see terribly well once she managed it—but what she *could* see was absolutely outrageous. Her top was shoved up as far as it would go, and his head was lowered to her all-but-bare breast, nuzzling it as she lay suspended between his hands at her shoulder blades and his erection, which was tucked up snugly against the juncture of her thighs.

When he found the tight, hard bud of one nipple and suckled it through the sleek fabric of her bra, she felt as if she'd just touched a live wire. A jolt of pure electricity surged through her, making her gasp as her back arched reflexively, pressing the sensitive region between her legs against the hard ridge beneath his fly. While the contact was unintentional, its impact was so tantalizing that, the next thing Julia knew, her legs were grappling for a tighter hold on his waist, and then she was rubbing against him . . . and she was doing it *deliberately*.

As if the shamelessly erotic act surprised him as much as it did her, his teeth closed sharply on her nipple for a fraction of an instant, hard enough to be painful if he hadn't released it so swiftly...and if she hadn't been so urgently, piercingly aroused that her addled mind registered that small nip as merely another variety of sensual stimulation. *Everything* was, at that point: the sound of their mingled raspy breathing; the smells of steam, his cologne and her own passion; and the pulsing pressure of his arousal against her as it continued to swell to very impressive proportions.

She groaned as he shifted her weight slightly, taking it on one hand and freeing the other to tug one of her bra's cups down below her breast, baring it. Though she relished the exquisite sensation of his fingers caressing her naked nipple, she fretted at the loss of the support that had enabled her to rub her lower body against him. Letting go of his nape, she dropped her hands behind her for better leverage, just as he, apparently, realized he'd deprived them of that pleasure. Returning his hand to her back, he drew her nipple back into his mouth and flicked the tip of his tongue across it, encouraging her to continue what she'd been doing.

"Oh, God, Chance . . ." Julia groaned, her head lolling back as she shivered and braced herself against the sensual onslaught of the two very different but complementary sensations: the caress of his mouth against her breast and the grinding friction of his denim-covered erection against the core of her femininity.

But the *third* sensation...? In her current state, it took her a moment for it to register at all, and, even then, she didn't understand it. Cold, hard and clammy against her fingers where they were splayed across the granite was just too different, too uncomplementary, to make sense.

Forcing her eyes open and turning her head, she peered down behind her, but, without her glasses, she couldn't see much more than vague suggestions of shapes and hazy colors. She recognized her fingers only because they were hers, and absently wondered if the object beside them was the lemon or the dish the potatoes had been in or...

And then, it *moved*.

4

JULIA'S HIGH-PITCHED CRY wasn't quite loud enough to qualify as a scream, but it was close enough to make Chance jerk his head up and open his eyes. Whatever had generated that noise, it certainly wasn't passion. As it turned out, it was a good thing he'd reacted that quickly. If she'd caught him off guard when she snatched her hands up from the counter and threw them around his neck, her momentum would have knocked them both over.

"Julia?" He grabbed her waist and struggled to balance her—or, more accurately, *them*—on the edge of the counter. It wasn't easy; she seemed determined not to touch any part of the granite, even if it meant climbing over him to get away from it. "What...?"

Still tenaciously clinging to him with all four limbs, her eyes glazed and her voice aghast, she told him, "It *moved*."

His penis? The earth? He knew for a fact that at least one of them had moved, but surely neither would have had her reacting like *this*. Neither would have had her looking over her shoulder, *behind* her, for that matter. Only...

Because her head blocked his view of the counter, he craned his neck to peer around it, following her gaze. He was chuckling even before she gasped and started scrambling to be released with every bit as much vigor as when she'd launched herself into his arms seconds earlier. Remarkable recovery time. Too remarkable; he'd thought he'd get to hold her a little longer.

"Damn," she muttered, glaring at the counter. Squinting at it, actually. She still didn't have her glasses—God, what *had* he done with them?—and it was obvious she couldn't see very well. "Is that what I think it is?"

"Larry the Lobster on the lam?" he offered, prompting her to glare at him as darkly as she had at the shellfish that had tried to get away... and probably would have made it, if he'd just been smart enough not to crawl across her hand.

"And how'd he get out of the bag in the first place?"

It was a good thing she couldn't see him smile. The demand sounded so haughty, but that effect was thoroughly undermined by her dishevelment...and by her attempts to pull herself together, all of which were so futile, they only made things worse.

Even though she'd yanked her top back down around her hips where it belonged, covering herself, he couldn't exactly say she was decent. Her bra's cup was still stretched below her breast, thrusting it up higher than the other, a lopsided condition that was even more noticeable with that aroused nipple jutting out so prominently against the soft velvet. He resisted the impulse to put everything back where he'd found it, since she didn't look as if she were in any mood to be convinced he had good intentions.

She looked mad—or *mortified*—enough to spit, and he was sure he didn't want to know which was actually the case. It was enough to watch her take it out on her hair, as she kept swiping at it in an attempt to put *it* back where it belonged. It was all too apparent that she wasn't going to succeed; between the steam and his hands, more of her hair was in a riotous froth around her face than was still tucked back in the braid. It really did seem like a living, independent, animate creature now—an absolutely breathtaking one, as a matter of fact.

And speaking of living, independent, animate creatures...

As he plucked the lobster off the counter and put it back in the sink with its less adventurous pal, Chance spied her glasses, which were dangling from a wire whisk in the spoon crock. Since he was neither brave or crazy enough to try helping with her bra, and he wasn't delusional enough to imagine he could help with her hair, the least he could do was let her see.

"Damn," she muttered again. "Where *are* my glasses?"

"Right here," he replied, carefully extracting them from the tangle of wire and wooden spoons and handing them over. As he did, he noticed how thick they really were. It was no wonder the lobster had startled her; she probably hadn't been able to tell what it was.

"I'll be so glad when I get rid of these things again," she grumbled as she put them back on.

"Rid of them?" he echoed blankly.

"Contacts. I'm getting fitted with new lenses, so I can't wear my old ones for two weeks."

"Oh." He liked the idea of being able to look right into her eyes, but it would take some getting used to; those big, serious tortoiseshell glasses were as much a part of the executive image as no-nonsense suits and lashed-down hair. On the other hand, he might not have any more trouble getting used to it than he'd had getting used to velvet sweat suits, lacy underwear or hell-gone-wild hair. He was kind of attached to all three of those things already.

Oh? That was all he had to say? Julia sincerely hoped he could do better than that. If she had to hold up both ends of the conversation by herself after what had just happened, she'd be ready for the men in white coats to cart her off to the psych unit at Bellevue by the time he left.

She'd certainly already exhibited clear signs of insanity. What else could she call it when she'd been going at it hot and heavy on a counter in a steamy kitchen with a virtual stranger, and all that had kept it from going any further was the timely intervention of a lobster on the loose?

Trying for normalcy even though her first shot at restoring it had been a dismal failure, she asked him to stick the butter in to melt while she took care of the lobsters. If she felt any guilt at not showing a little more gratitude toward her rescuer, it was offset by her anticipation of how relieved she'd feel once she disposed of the witnesses.

"There's still water left in that pot?"

So much for normalcy, she thought, turning redder than the lobsters would once they were cooked. She wished the floor would simply open up and swallow her, removing her from this impossible situation before she made an even bigger fool of herself. She wished he'd stop smiling at her with that expression of tolerant amusement and drop the subject. Most of all, however, she wished she could just hand him the damned lobsters and tell him to take 'em home to Quakertown.

Oh, no, she didn't.

If this wasn't insanity, she didn't know what was. She'd never been so irritated, embarrassed and aroused in her life—and all at one time, too. It was no wonder she'd also never been more confused.

"Julia?" he asked softly.

"Yes?" She looked up warily, reminding herself that a *Julia* spoken just like that had been her downfall.

"Y'all're trying to pretend it never happened, aren't you?"

She could deny it, but had enough sense left not to think he'd believe her. And, in all truth, she wasn't trying to pretend it had never happened; she was trying to *forget* it.

"You can't, you know."

Pretend or forget? she wondered absently, though she knew it didn't matter. She wouldn't be able to manage either of them any time in the foreseeable future . . . if ever.

He closed in on her then, so close, she could feel the heat radiating from his body, and her powerful urge to be drawn to it was nearly as hard to resist as her urge to flee. Just when she thought she'd stood her ground long enough to prove she could, he finally spoke, his voice as low, cool and mesmerizing as his words were low, hot and positively scandalizing.

"I'm not gonna let you pretend you weren't up there on that countertop with your legs wrapped around me, hanging on tight and kissing me while you were working on building up enough friction to start a fire."

He stepped even closer, nearly touching her. While proving she could stand her ground was so far removed from her mind, it wasn't even in the picture anymore, she was now frozen in place, unable to move or speak or even breathe.

"And I'm not gonna let you pretend you weren't hot and wet, because I felt it—the same way you could feel I was hard then, and still am now."

As if she had any doubts about his readiness, he grabbed her hand and pressed it to the fly of his jeans, the implication that he might prove the corollary the same way plain in his eyes. She snatched her hand back before he could—and he let it go—but he'd already made his point.

"And I'm not gonna let you pretend that you didn't like it when I was sucking your nipple...."

Through the fabric of her top, he hooked his finger in the edge of her bra, easing it out from her body far enough for her breast to slide inside, and she dragged a ragged breath into her lungs, certain it was going to be her last.

"...or that you weren't so close to coming, you were making breathy little noises and trembling and calling my name...."

He dragged his thumb across her breast just above her hard nipple, and she shuddered reflexively, her hands clenching into fists at her sides.

"... or that you wouldn't have been perfectly willing—no, make that *eager*—to make love with me, right then and there, if that damned lobster hadn't gotten out of the sink."

Raising his hand, he cradled her jaw in the vee between his thumb and his fingers, his pinkie resting on the place where she could feel her pulse pounding furiously.

"And I'm not gonna let you pretend that we aren't gonna make love, because it's gonna happen—not tonight, but soon—just as sure as you and I are standing here right now."

JULIA FULLY EXPECTED to hear Denise knocking on her door the instant Chance left, and she wasn't disappointed. She wished she had been, actually, because this was one time when she really *was* in no mood to have to concede that someone else was right.

It had been bad enough that Chance had been satisfied making her squirm. Which she *had*...all through preparing dinner, eating it at the pretty table she'd set for her and Barth the night before, and drinking their coffee in front of the fire afterward. She'd kept waiting for him to bring the subject up again, dreading it until she'd been ready to scream.

He hadn't, though. Not even when he'd kissed her good-night on his way out the door—a little first-date kind of kiss that hadn't involved anything hot, wet, or hard. After all the torrid images that had paraded through her mind during the course of the evening, she'd had a tough time making up her mind whether to be disappointed or relieved by his restraint.

To her regret, she'd decided she was both.

"Well?" Denise demanded as soon as she was settled on the sofa with a cup from a fresh pot of coffee and a leftover slice of double-chocolate, *framboise* torte.

"Well, what?" Julia bluffed, hoping to delay the inevitable for another couple seconds. She figured ten, at best, but she could try.

"Don't you give me that, girl. I saw him at the office, and he's one major hunk. Rachel's very put out that he came *here* for dinner, and she has every right to be."

"So we had dinner. I had an extra lobster, remember?"

"Right." Denise fixed her see-all golden cat's-eye stare on Julia, who felt herself beginning to squirm all over again. "And I'm the tooth fairy in my spare time. You didn't light that cozy fire so the two of you could get a better look at the battle plan for the campaign."

Julia flushed uncontrollably, and Denise crowed.

"You *didn't*. Julia, didn't your mama teach you any better'n to do things like that on the first date?"

"I *didn't* . . . and it wasn't a date."

"If he kissed you good-night, it was a date."

Unable to deny the accusation, Julia felt her face heat up even more.

"I knew it." Denise grinned smugly. "Nice to see you with a real man, for a change."

"Barth's . . ."

"Barth's *boring*. And he's a pompous idiot, and he's got a vastly over-inflated opinion of himself and . . ."

"And he's losing his hair," Julia conceded halfheartedly.

"That, too, but that's not his fault, it's lousy genes. On his mother's side, I think." Denise set her empty plate on the cocktail table, tucked her longer-than-eternity legs beneath her and sighed. "So, what, exactly, kept the boy wonder out of the picture tonight?"

"Taking the troops from Starways out on the town."

"Just goes to show what an idiot he is. Busting his buns on that job, and the company's gonna fold, no matter what he does."

Julia couldn't say anything against Barth on that account; she'd been guilty of doing the same thing—more than once—on equally doomed projects.

"It's not the same thing, and you know it," Denise told her, clearly reading her mind. "There's a world of difference between making Sugar Tips and Ranger look like good ideas and giving them a shot at making it, and trying to gull the public into playing 'forgive and forget' with a proven loser like Starways. At least nobody ever died from edible fingernails or smelling bad."

"Nobody's *smelled* Ranger yet," Julia reasonably pointed out.

"And, by the time they do, you'll have them convinced men're supposed to smell that way."

"God forbid."

"Or that they'll look like Chance Palladin if they use it." Denise smiled fiendishly, back to a topic that interested her a great deal more than the dubious ethics of advertising. "I told you that wasn't professional ambition I saw lurking in your eyes. It was good, old fashioned lust."

Denise was right . . . again. Would it kill Julia to admit it one more time?

"Not that I'm saying there's anything wrong with it, mind you," Denise amended. "There's nothing that gets the juices flowing and reminds a woman she's still alive like indulging in a little X-rated fantasy every now and then. The only adequate substitute for fantasy—not sufficient, but adequate—is food, and you don't have the metabolism to burn up calories the way I can."

Close enough. The reminder that she had to watch what she ate was a dirty shot, though.

"Got any more of that cake?"

Long after she'd booted Denise back up to her own apartment and ended a predictably vague and awkward telephone conversation with Barth—who had been home from his night out with the boys from Starways well before the clock struck midnight—Julia was still prowling restlessly around her apartment, unable to sleep. Another glass of wine, a nice hot cup of cocoa, another slice of torte—not the best combination, back to back—and working on the campaign schedule in front of the last dregs of the fire hadn't helped, either. If anything, it had only made the problem worse. Every time she'd realized exactly how much time she was going to be spending with Chance in the next few months, the odds of her getting to sleep at all dropped another couple of notches.

If it were just a good old-fashioned case of guilt that was getting to her, it would make things so much simpler. Certainly, being eaten up with remorse for how close she'd come to betraying Barth, forgiving herself and vowing not to do it again—which would be the decent way to feel right now, she supposed—would be a lot less complicated than the way she genuinely felt. She wasn't the least bit remorseful and she couldn't see any point in forgiving herself for something she had every intention of doing again, given the opportunity. She'd make one, if necessary.

She didn't think it would come to that, however. Chance had made it quite clear that he was willing—no, make that *eager*—to pick up where they'd left off, sometime very, very soon. At the time, she'd been too embarrassed by her disgraceful behavior for it to sink in that he'd not only liked it, but had been as aroused and out of control as she. If she'd never acted like that before in her life, with any man—and she hadn't—no man had ever been like that with her before, either. And she liked it, too . . . a lot. Enough to get over her embarrassment and get on with the real cause of her sleeplessness—the two-fisted punch of unfulfilled desire and anticipation. The way she felt, she wasn't going to get any sleep until they did make love.

And, in the meantime, she thought there was still another slice or two of that double-chocolate, *framboise* torte left in the refrigerator. . . .

THE FOLLOWING MORNING, uncharacteristically, Chance found Maggie and Amanda, his receptionist and hygienist, both already in his office, well into their morning routines, by the time he arrived. He'd known he was running late, but having Amanda get there before him proved just how late he was. As often as not, he was with his first patient before she blew in. Not that he held it against her; as a divorced mother of three, she had her hands full at home. From the sounds of things, he thought it was impressive that she ever managed to make it in at all.

This time, he beat the first patient by a matter of seconds, which didn't give him much time to breathe, let alone enough time for his usual cup of coffee. Thankfully, it didn't give Maggie and Amanda time to grill him about being late, either. With less than three hours' sleep to his credit, he was in no condition to come up with a quick explanation for the lapse.

The truth? Not hardly. Sure, he'd be willing to tell them he'd overslept, but not how it had happened. Even he thought it reflected poorly on his sanity that, as soon as he'd walked into his house after the long drive back from New York, he'd suddenly been seized by an unaccountable impulse to build a fire. It had taken him so long to do it—damp wood, all the way down to the tinder—he'd then felt obliged to sit up and enjoy it for a while. Three beers later, he'd finally acknowledged that he was still there because he was just too restless to sleep.

Restless? Is that what he was calling it these days, or had he picked it up from someone who never came out and said what she really meant? The fact was, he'd been up half the night, staring into the smoldering fire and trying to convince himself he ought to get some sleep before it was time to get up, because he'd been hornier than a stag in rut.

Yep, he guessed that pretty well summed it up. For himself, anyway. He'd have to come up with something less...descriptive for Maggie and Amanda. Considering that old Mr. Walbert was only coming in for a cleaning and a checkup—and half his teeth came out and got scrubbed with a good hard brush every night—he had no more than twenty minutes to come up with a decent excuse.

Amanda didn't give him that long. Ten minutes later, as he was picking at the plaque between Mr. Walbert's bottom incisors, she casually remarked, "So, what happened, Chance? You take the day off and forget you have a job to get up for in the morning?"

It was pointless for him to hope his protective glasses hid the flash of panic in his eyes, since his hand twitched—just once, but hard enough to draw blood. As Mr. Walbert squawked in wordless protest, the expression in his eyes mirrored Chance's own. "Sorry 'bout that, Mr. Walbert. My hand slipped."

"'O pwob'em," the man replied, doing his best to talk around the pick and several of Chance's gloved fingers.

"I was in New York yesterday, got back late and overslept," Chance explained, carefully skirting along the edge of the truth without actually treading on it.

"I yike 'ew Yo'k," Mr. Walbert contributed. "'E go do Wadio Thidy Yuthic 'all e'wy yeah do thee the Wockeths i' th' Cwithmuth Thow."

Translating the comment with the ease of a man who'd gotten used to holding just such garbled conversations, Chance answered, "I've never been to Radio City or seen the Rockettes. Maybe next Christmas. I went up there to talk to a woman at an ad agency."

"An ad agency?" Amanda echoed, the pitch of her voice rising half an octave in astonishment. "After everything you said about it being tacky for medical people to advertise anywhere but the yellow pages, you're considering running ads, anyway?"

"It *is* tacky," he assured her. "And I'm not...."

"I hope to God you're not thinking about TV," she continued. "All you can afford's very late night and cable, and, I'm warning you right now, I'll quit before I see us in the middle of an "All in the Family" rerun, sandwiched between the Ginzu knives and some 900 phone-sex number. Can you imagine the kind of calls we'll get from people who're too drunk or stupid to figure out where one ad ends and the next one begins?"

"You can relax, Amanda. Even if I could afford it— which I can't, even in late night—I'm not thinking about advertising the practice."

"Oh." She finally breathed, in relief and out of necessity, he was sure. "So then, why'd you go up to see this woman at the ad agency?"

"She wants me to do commercials for some new men's cologne."

Chance had spent the past five days dreading the moment when he'd have to admit that fact to Amanda and Maggie. He'd had good reason to; Amanda's reaction exceeded his worst fears by miles.

"Cologne?"

Until that moment, he'd forgotten his own first reaction to the idea, but Amanda reminded him. She was laughing so hard, it was a good thing it wasn't *her* hands in Mr. Walbert's mouth.

"C'mon, now, Amanda . . ." he contended, finding himself in the unlikely position of defending an idea he'd deemed equally absurd—and too rattled to appreciate the irony in it. "Is it really so funny?"

Her head moved up and down violently as she forced out the only word she could manage. "Cologne?"

"'Oor gonna be un of dothe pwethy boyth id de magathi'es?" Mr. Walbert asked. Sighing with resignation, Chance decided he might as well let them both have their say—and get it out of their systems—and removed his hands and the pick from the old man's mouth. "Like that guy with all the muscles who does the ads for that perfume in those skimpy little French swimsuits?"

"I won't be wearing a swimsuit." He hoped, anyway. He hadn't asked, but it didn't sound like something that would go along with the Western motif.

"You gonna be buck naked, Doc?" Mr. Walber wanted to know, aghast and fascinated at the same time. "Like that . . ."

"Cologne?" Amanda repeated, clearly unable to get past that concept.

"I'm not gonna be naked, either." Again, he hoped. Western didn't necessarily preclude that, but she was talking about snow, and, as far as he was concerned, snow ruled nudity out. "It's called Ranger, so they're going with a Western theme—jeans and boots, guns and cowboy hats, horses . . . that sort of thing."

"Like them Marlboro ads, from back when they could still run ads for cigarettes on TV?"

"Cologne?"

"Something like that, I think. I . . ."

Chance couldn't finish what he was saying, but neither could anyone else, as a shrill scream carried in from the waiting room. He gave it a minute for his heart to settle back down out of his throat, and glanced at Amanda for confirmation as he guessed, "We got the Campbell kid up next? And his mother's still not telling him where he's going till she gets him here?"

Collecting herself admirably, she replied, "He *is* scheduled for today, and it sounds like it."

"Oh, Lord." And Maggie hadn't had a chance to get her digs in yet, either. It was going to be a very long day.

He didn't know the half of it, as it turned out to be a very long *week*. The longest week of Chance's lifetime, by the time it was through. It wasn't enough for Maggie and Amanda to give him endless grief about his "glamorous" new job themselves; they had to tell all his patients about it, too. Within a matter of days, he was getting it from everyone, including the checkout woman at the grocery store, and wondering exactly what he'd been thinking when he'd agreed to become the Ranger Man.

Which was, of course, the other reason the week had seemed so long. At least a half-dozen times a day, he'd wanted to call Julia—alternating between wanting to tell her to forget it and wanting to tell her he missed her—but he'd talked himself out of it every time. When the thought of the money couldn't do it, he had to remind himself that all he had was her work number. If he called it, he was just as apt to get Rachel, whom he didn't want to encourage, or find Barth, whom he wanted to encourage to get lost, hanging around her office. Either way, he'd only make himself crazy, since what he really wanted was to see Julia, hold her in his arms and kiss her until they both lost control.

And he intended to do just that as soon as he saw her again—so much for the idea of quitting—when he went back up to New York in only a few more days. . . .

THOUGH HE COULDN'T SEE a thing outside the circle of bright light, Chance knew the instant Julia stepped into the studio. He felt it, with the same undefinable sixth sense that had told him, back in his oil days, when a big strike was hidden just a little deeper beneath the surface. He'd almost be willing to claim he smelled her out there in the shadows, even if he recognized, on a rational level, that the only scents in the air were those of hot lights, dust, and darkroom chemicals.

Despite the stern order from Geoff Logan, the photographer, not to move a muscle until they'd finished arranging the lights, Chance was compelled to peer into the dark corner where he knew she was standing, and he had to lift his head a fraction of an inch to do it. He had only enough time for his eyes to adjust to the gloom, pick out the compact silhouette of her head and note that her hair was all fastened down again—but, this time, how?—before Geoff caught him at it.

"C'mon, mate," the Australian chastised him, sighing as if Chance had just violated some sacred law. "Have a heart, there. These folks're all gettin' paid by the hour, but I'm only gettin' paid once, no matter how long it takes."

"These folks" were the photographer's assistant, the makeup and hair stylists, the female model and another woman who, as far as he could determine, did nothing but clutch a clipboard to her chest, chainsmoke, and yell a lot.

"Far as that goes, you're not workin' on the clock, either, so I'd think you'd want to get outta here as soon as you can."

And he did. For that matter, he'd been ready to get out of there since shortly after Geoff had started in on the second roll of black and whites of him alone. He'd begun chomping at the bit in earnest about the same time the model had been added to the picture. Still black-and-white at that point, although they'd finally moved on to the wonderful world of color a half hour ago.

So far, Geoff had taken his picture with a shirt on, with a hat on, with the shirt *and* hat on, without a shirt *or* hat, both with *and* without the model . . . and with a cushy leather chair . . . a potted saguaro cactus . . . a Texas-sized Lone Star flag . . . and the biggest, ugliest painting he'd ever seen depicting the siege of the Alamo—short of the huge, godawful one that was actually in the Mission itself.

"Down just a bit more," Geoff directed Chance, referring to the position of his head. "We want the light to cut across your cheeks, keeping your eyes in the shadow of the hat and the lower half of your face fully lit." After Chance made three more minor adjustments and the photographer was satisfied, he gestured toward the model. "You there, luv—what's your name again?—come on back in now. Right hand on his chest . . . no, the other side . . . left behind your back with the Ranger bottle . . . no, luv, with the label facing *this* way . . . That's it. Don't anyone *move.*"

From her refuge in the shadowy corner, Julia watched Chance slouch against the fake adobe wall, looking as if he were waiting for the rest of the posse to gather so they could go out looking for cattle rustlers or whatever it was posses hunted these days. Though every muscle in his body was at ease, a tautness remained that was, apparently, an integral part of his being.

"He's really a natural, isn't he?" whispered Damian, the photographer's assistant, as he joined her.

"He certainly is." He had one ankle propped casually atop the other, stretching the faded denim of his jeans over muscular thighs, and his arms were crossed over his midriff, straining the fabric of his shirt across an equally powerful pair of shoulders. Unreasonably, she found herself resenting the model for blocking her view.

And, even more unreasonably, for touching him. Her hand was slipped inside the half-open placket of his shirt, lying flat on the smooth curve between his collarbone and his nipple, and Julia was far too agitated by the sight to recognize that it was there because Geoff had ordered her to put it there.

"So, that's another roll, then," Geoff announced a short time later, setting aside the camera. "You've got fifteen to hit the loo or snag a cigarette or whatever you like. Long as you're back in time, I won't ask."

Beside Julia, Damian, who had things to do during the break, jumped to attention. Though he told her goodbye as he headed on his way, Julia barely noticed. She was too busy watching Chance as he levered himself away from the backdrop, using only the muscles in his legs, rather than the ones in his hands and arms, to propel himself to an upright position. Those muscles didn't just *look* powerful; they really *were*, as if he did all the things she associated with cowboys—like spend his days in the saddle, busting broncos and roping dogies, and his nights in the saloon, kicking up his heels and knocking the ladies dead.

As he started toward her, his hat cocked down over the front of his face, he walked with that distinctive rolling boot-shod gait, and the image of the cowboy was stronger than ever. It was all too easy to forget that, in actual fact, Chance Palladin spent his days filling cavities and lecturing on the benefits of proper flossing and brushing.

And, in the moment when he stepped out of the light and into the shadow, closing in on her, Julia did forget.

Leaving the harsh white light of the photographer's set for the near-total darkness surrounding it momentarily blinded Chance, but he kept moving forward, anyway. His eyes would adjust to the change soon enough, and, in the meantime, he was confident he'd know, somehow, how much distance was between them, just like a night-hunting animal can rely on its other senses to compensate for its lack of sight and pinpoint its prey in the dark.

Whether his senses were really that finely honed or he just got lucky, he couldn't say for sure; either way, he stopped short of running into her. He was so close, it was no longer merely an illusion that he could smell her. His automatic response to that unique blend of hundred-dollar-an-ounce perfume and that special scent that was hers alone was so overwhelming that, even once his vision was restored, the sight of the dress-for-success suit and the no-nonsense hair—up again, this time in some sort of twist that put him in mind of a doughnut—didn't spark a single image of Julia as a marginally female female executive anymore.

Far from it. Now that he'd already seen her lacy underwear, he was less likely to be put off by her man-tailored suit than he was to wonder what she was wearing under it. Now that he'd heard her cry out in passion, he couldn't be fooled by that austere businesslike facade. And, now that he'd felt her writhe in his arms, threatening to come apart at any instant, he was too impatient to restrain his behavior in front of an audience, so he pulled her out into the hall where they could be alone.

It was lighter out there, but not light enough to blind him again, so he could see that she didn't look as though she had any objections to his presumption. In fact, the expression on her face suggested that she would have dragged him out there herself, if he'd hesitated another couple of seconds. As far as he could remember—and he was sure something so unforgettable couldn't have slipped his mind—no other woman had ever looked at him in exactly that way: with such rapt intensity, it felt as though she were trying to absorb every detail in order to imprint him on her very soul.

That singleminded regard was so compelling, Chance wasn't just willing to let her claim him with her eyes, mind and soul; he *wanted* her to do it, and he wanted it enough to make it easier for her. Ignoring the nagging sensation that there was something not quite right about that desire—something he couldn't quite define, but felt all the same—he took one step closer, then another, until she was backed against the wall and his chest was pressed against her lapels.

Groaning her name, he lowered his mouth to hers. It was as sweet as he remembered, as seductively hot and moist, promising myriad glorious pleasures that made his wildest fantasies seem pallid in comparison. He'd had a lot of them in the last week—enough to ensure that he'd built a fire practically every night and then sat up well into the wee hours of the morning, staring into it. He'd stopped calling that perpetually gnawing need that was keeping him awake "restlessness" four days earlier.

"I missed you," he whispered against the side of her throat, at a more comfortable height, now that she had heels on.

"And here I thought it was the gun," Julia teased, running her finger up the prop holster from his thigh and following the belt around his hips to the back. Slipping her hands into his back pockets, she cupped them over his buttocks and pulled his pelvis more snugly against hers.

"If y'all don't stop that," he warned her, "we're both gonna have to call in sick for the rest of the day and go to your place to recuperate."

To his relief—and regret—her fingers eased out of his pockets and retreated up to safer territory on his back.

"Can't," she softly insisted, shaking her head.

"Can't or won't?"

"Can't," she repeated, with a little more conviction. "Big meeting this afternoon."

5

"THE HEAD HONCHOS from Ranger again?" Chance asked, absently stroking her thigh and finding the unmistakable ridge of a garter under her slim skirt. Spontaneously, the discovery triggered a mental picture of Julia, clad in a lacy bra, a garter belt, and stockings . . . and nothing else. That image didn't do a thing to bolster either his limited concentration or his flagging self-control.

"Bigger than Ranger. Much bigger." For a moment, he wasn't entirely sure she was talking about an ad campaign, but then she went on, "Hale and Hearty—a bakery that manufactures bread and cookies over in Jamaica—is planning on going national. . . ."

"You mean international, don't you?"

With a little laugh that he felt more than heard, she added, "Jamaica, the train station on the other side of Brooklyn . . . not Jamaica, the island on the other side of Cuba."

"Oh." He'd have to take her word for it, at least until he found a map.

"Anyway, the plan is for them to be distributing regionwide by the end of this year, and nationwide by the end of next . . . and they want *me* to handle the launch."

"Congratulations. Sounds like a big job. A job too big for you to be tackling it with the assistant with no brain." As well as being too big for her to have any time left over—for him or anything else, Chance groused,

even as his conscience accused him of being childish and
selfish, when he ought to be pleased at her success, instead.

"By the time this campaign gets rolling, I won't be
working with Rachel anymore."

Julia's smile changed into something he could only
describe as predatory, and, for an instant, the far-
fetched notion that she was planning to kill Rachel to
get rid of her crossed his mind. He recognized how ridiculous it was even before it was suppressed by the
knowledge that she didn't need to resort to such a cold-
blooded solution; all she had to do was serve out her
time, and a couple of months wasn't *that* long to wait.
"That's right. What is it—a hundred days now?"

"Ninety-five, as of today. Except . . ."

"You found a husband for Rachel?"

"Better than that. I negotiated a trial contract with
Hale and Hearty, and it's only for six months."

He frowned, genuinely confused. "That's good?"

She grinned, genuinely elated. "It's *great*. It means
they aren't committed to sticking out a long contract
when I bolt from Locke, Reade and Hutchinson."

"You're getting a new job? Who's gonna handle
Ranger after that?" Barth? God, he hoped not. At least
with Julia running this dog-and-pony show, he had
better-than-even odds of coming out of it with some of
his dignity intact. If Barth took over, he could pretty
well give up any hope of that.

"*I* will. Still be handling Ranger, that is. But I won't
be doing it for Locke, Reade and Hutchinson. It'll be for
myself."

"You're gonna start your own agency?" Chance demanded, and then lowered his voice conspiratorially.

"Can you do that? Take Ranger and Hale and Hearty with you, I mean? Is that legal?"

"Once their contracts are up, if they want to go with me and no one can prove I lured them away while I was still working for the agency, I can." That look was still there, in her smile and in her eyes. He could call it predatory and cold-blooded, or he could call it confident; either way, Julia Adams was one very ambitious lady.

"No guts, no glory," she told him, lifting her shoulders in a shrug that was appealing enough to sway him toward confidence, which didn't sound as grim. "If I stay where I am, the prospects are awfully bleak. There're so many partners already, I won't be far enough up the totem pole to get an office with a window until the year 2017."

"Or have somebody below you to stick with the next assistant from hell," Chance added, telling himself that there was nothing wrong with confidence, and she did have a point that went deeper than a window or her choice of assistant. He'd already figured out that advertising was even more competitive than oil had been. If she wanted to succeed, she had to play by *their* rules, instead of the stricter ones that governed the rest of the world. "Maybe you can give Rachel to Barth when you leave, and they can finish Starways off together."

"Too late," Julia said, her laugh sounding more amazed than amused. "Don't you ever read the paper? Watch TV?"

"Lately, I haven't had a lot of extra time. Why?"

"Starways shut down operations at midnight last Thursday, and then filed for bankruptcy as soon as the federal courthouse opened its doors the next morning. Sold tickets right up until the last minute, leaving a lot of people royally pissed-off over being stranded without a flight . . . or even a company rep to yell at about it."

Chance had still had enough time to watch the news back when Continental had done the same thing a few years earlier. Judging by what he'd seen then, he was sure every airport in the country must have had its share of ugly scenes, and . . . "So, how's Barth taking it?"

"A lot better now, but when the Starways folks showed up in the office on Thursday morning . . ."

"Oh, God . . . that's right. They were in New York."

"Stranded, like everybody else with Starways tickets. They didn't know it was coming, either, until *they* saw it on the news. And, because Starways pulled all their company credit cards when they snuck off into the night, they couldn't even book a flight back home with somebody else."

"So much for flying the friendly skies." Though he felt bad for the people—passengers *and* employees—who'd gotten caught in the sudden collapse of Starways, Chance felt a wicked sense of glee that Barth had had the rug snatched out from under him, too. He'd been so sure he'd be able to save them—so damnably cocky about it—and he'd been wrong.

Which just went to show the other thing he'd already figured out about advertising: it was every bit as risky as oil, with big payoffs or big busts and nothing in between. If she could handle that, too—if she really believed that "no guts, no glory" was the fast track to success—more power to her; by the time he'd hung up his hard hat and gloves, he'd reached the point that the mere idea of taking one more risk had been enough to put him in a cold sweat, and he'd been glad to change his tune to "better safe than sorry."

"So, let's go out tonight and celebrate your big coup with Hale and Hearty. I didn't drive into the city this time—I took your advice and took the bus."

"Can't," she told him again, with a pained expression on her face.

They were back to this, it seemed. "Can't or won't?"

"Can't. I'm going to a cocktail party and buffet...."

"Oh. I didn't bring any other clothes with me this time, either." He brushed his knuckles across the downy skin of her cheek, hoping she'd tell him she didn't really want to go to this party, but would rather spend the evening alone with him. They could light a fire, call out for Chinese delivery, and let things go where they would after that. He had a few suggestions—and protection, just in case. "Just my jeans, so I couldn't...."

"...with Barth," she finished reluctantly.

So, that explained the pained expression on her face. Not just that she planned to spend the evening with Barth—though, God knew, that would be enough to make anybody cringe—but that she hadn't wanted him to know about it. Reining in a reaction he knew overstepped the boundaries of a relationship that hadn't yet been defined, Chance calmly asked, "Oh?"

As soon as she'd admitted she was seeing Barth that night, Julia wished she hadn't. For that matter, she wished she hadn't *had* to admit it. And she wouldn't have, if she'd just had enough sense—and enough backbone—to tell Barth she didn't want to go to this party, after all. Though they'd made the plans almost a month earlier, it wasn't as if she'd written it in her calendar in *ink*. If she'd canceled, he would have understood, just as he always did.

She hadn't, though. God alone knew why, since she certainly didn't. It wasn't as if she hadn't thought about it a half-dozen times—or more—in the last few days.

"I... We..." Julia also didn't know why she was having so much trouble answering Chance. For a woman who could ordinarily think so well on her feet, she was appalled to discover that she suddenly couldn't think at all. She was simply too flustered to come up with anything, let alone something sensible, to say. The best she could manage was, "I..."

"Yes?" he prompted. If he'd meant it to be helpful, it had precisely the opposite effect. The same applied to the hand that rubbed her thigh through her skirt, tracking down the inside edge of her garter to where it was clipped to the top of her stocking, and then back up the outside to her hip.

"We..."

Chance sighed, and it was more than a sound; Julia could see the look of disappointment in his eyes, feel the slow fall of his chest against hers before he said, "You can't mean to tell me you actually want to go out with Barth, can you, Julia?"

She couldn't, of course. She did manage to find her voice and sputter out, "It's one of those charity things. I said I'd go a month ago, when he bought the tickets."

It was obvious that the fact that the event was for charity had less of an impact on Chance than the point that she'd agreed to the date a month earlier, *before* he and Julia had met. *Before* they'd kissed. *Before* she'd been well on her way to being naked in his arms, practically begging him to make love to her. It was little consolation, she could tell, but it did have the effect of reminding him how briefly they'd known each other. In spite of everything that had happened between them the night he'd been at her apartment for dinner, they really didn't know each other well enough for him to be entitled to demand explanations from her or object to her date with Barth.

She felt him chafing at that awareness and then he swallowed and took several deep breaths, collecting himself before asking, in a carefully guarded voice, "How late do you think y'all might be at this charity thing?"

"Well, these aren't like real parties, where everybody comes fashionably late. Instead, the whole point is to show up early, touch base with everyone you want to know you were there, and get out before they start making speeches congratulating one another for saving civilization as we know it. The last time we went to one, we were out the door by eleven o'clock." Noting the still-contentious look on Chance's face, Julia prudently skated around the issue of where they'd gone or what they'd done after that; it had been one of Barth's better attempts at being romantic, with candles and wine and ... "On a weeknight, my guess is maybe ten, since everyone's got to get up for work tomor—"

"Hey, Palladin!" Damian yelled, poking his head out the door into the hall. "Geoff wants to know if your watch stopped, or if you thought he was just kidding when he said fifteen minutes."

"He told me to take off my watch, remember? Said a digital was too cosmopolitan for a cowboy," Chance reminded him, holding up his arm to show his bare wrist. "Tell him I'll be right in."

"Sure thing," Damian called back, before retreating into the studio.

"Call me when you get in?" Chance asked Julia, clearly aware that he didn't have much time, so he had to hurry. "Don't worry, I'll still be up."

He sounded as if he had no doubts about that, and she wanted to smile. She couldn't explain exactly why. Maybe because it suggested that he was having as much trouble getting to sleep as she was herself? "Sure, I'll call. Do I have your . . . ?"

"Got a pen?"

With a nod, Julia began digging in her purse and finally unearthed a ballpoint; her *good* pen—a Montblanc fountain pen she kept in her desk and used only on special occasions, like contract and bonus-check signings—had been Barth's birthday gift to her two years earlier. Handing the ballpoint to Chance, she plunged back into her purse, this time hunting for her address book . . . or at least a scrap of paper.

Before she found either, his hand skimmed up the length of her thigh, sliding beneath her skirt as he pushed its hem almost to her hip . . . in the process, baring the skin between the top of her stocking and the leg of her panties. Still gripping the flap of her purse with one hand and keeping the other one inside, she turned her head and looked down to see what he was doing.

He wouldn't! Julia told herself, too stunned to move or even protest. *He isn't!*

But he would, and he was; as a matter of fact, he already *had*. Emblazoned across her upper thigh, in figures more than an inch high, was a ten-digit number, complete with parentheses and a dash setting off the first two three-digit segments. As Chance finished the last numeral in what could only be his phone number, he lifted his head to look up at her and grin, too mischievously for her to be mad at him.

"And to think I spent all that money on a Rolodex," she told him dryly.

He shook his head and went back to admiring his handiwork. "More than one'd be pretty gaudy, I think. You'd look like the tattooed lady at the circus."

"I don't now?"

"It's not as if I put it where just anyone can see it," he told her, rising to his feet and letting her skirt drop to cover it. "See?"

Before she could come up with an answer for that— if there was one, which she genuinely doubted—he leaned down to drop a quick kiss on her lips, handed back her pen, and set off for the studio again. Before the door swung shut behind him, he smiled at her one last time and said, "Until tonight, then. I'll be waiting up."

THE NEXT TIME JULIA saw Chance, a week later, he was still grinning like a cat who had just heisted his owner's canary right out of its cage . . . and was now eyeing the fish tank as if he were thinking about having guppies for dessert.

So, what could that mean? That he *knew* she'd told Barth she had to put in a call to the West Coast by six-thirty, their time, in order to get home from the party and get rid of him in time to call Chance by quarter after ten, long before an hour that could be considered "waiting up"? Or that he *knew* she hadn't been able to go to the gym for the last week because the label on the Cross pen's refill hadn't been lying when it said "indelible"? Or that he *knew* she hadn't gotten more than a dozen hours' sleep in the last seven days and was secretly praying she wouldn't get much more than that during the next five, while they were up in Canada shooting "snow pictures" for the Christmas ads?

God, she hoped not.

"That's him?" asked Eric Kistler, the director in charge of the TV ads. He tipped his head to one side, studying Chance from across the distance of the airline's waiting room, as if mentally walking him through each of the ads' scenarios. As Chance rose from the molded-plastic seat—orange, of the type indigenous to airports and emergency waiting rooms—flashed her a smile, and leaned down to hook his fingers through the strap of his duffel bag, Eric murmured, more to himself than to Julia, "Moves well, too. Graceful, but nothing overt about it."

"If he just weren't a *blonde*," griped Dominick Scarpino, the cameraman, as Chance sauntered toward them, his stride casual but confident. "That snow glare's gonna be enough of a bitch, and you had to pick a guy who doesn't even have a little contrast to make it easier?"

"Work with it, Dom," Julia told him, her fingers tightening on the grip of her suitcase. He'd been grumbling about one thing or another ever since they'd gotten in the limo back in the city. He always did, though, so she ought to be used to it. "He's not gonna get any darker, and I'm not going out looking for another one with dark hair, just to suit you. It was hard enough finding him, you know."

"If you ask me," muttered Dom, "we're doin' this whole thing the hard way. Goin' clear up to *Canada* to find snow?"

"Got a better idea? It's March." The first week, and still bitterly cold—but snowless, as most of the winter had been.

He narrowed his eyes at her balefully. "Don't you ever read the paper? Watch TV?"

"Now where've I heard that before?" Chance commented, as he got close enough to hear.

"What do the papers and TV have to do with going to Canada, anyway?" she demanded of Dom, once she'd finished introducing the three men. "The last time I checked, Canada wasn't in any danger of being taken over by gun-toting revolutionaries with foreigner-seeking bullets."

"Like when we were down in Grenada, working on those ads for Lime'n Cola?" Dom reminded her, his eyes gleaming. "You remember that, don't you, Julia? We were trapped in Hutchinson's cousin's villa for three whole days before the marines landed."

"Right. A real hardship, if ever I saw one," Julia pointed out, noting the way Chance was looking at Dom—one tomcat to another, much the same way he'd looked at Barth during that first meeting in her office. Surely, he didn't think that she and Dom were some sort of hot item, just because they'd been in Grenada together? What did he think she did, anyway—maintain a string of men for her own amusement? "Being trapped inside a compound with a twelve-foot wall, a swimming pool, and a wine cellar that would've made the sommelier at Lutèce sick with envy."

"*Would've* being the operative word," the cameraman confided to Chance. "But only because we had to prevent them from falling into enemy hands, of course."

"Of course," Chance soberly agreed, relaxing in apparent recognition of the fact that the relationship between her and Dom was friendly but purely professional.

"Cases and cases of the best France ever had to offer," Eric muttered disgruntledly. "Just there for the drinking, and I had to miss it."

"So, who told you to go and have your gallbladder taken out that week?" Dom asked.

"My internist. It was emergency surgery, remember?"

"Was there some reason y'all were asking if Julia'd read the paper or watched TV?" Chance asked, smoothly deflecting the topic back to its original course. "Far as I can tell, *this* airline's still in business. Is it in some kind of trouble I just haven't heard about?"

"Only the same trouble every other airline's gonna be up to their wings in this weekend, when the big storm hits."

"Storm?" Chance echoed.

"Storm, my behind," Eric scoffed. "They've been predicting a big storm every other weekend since October, and I haven't seen enough snow yet to build a decent snowman. If I believed it this time, I'd be back in the city making plans to shoot these ads in Central Park, not on my way up to White Moose in Canada."

"White *Elk*," Dom corrected him. "And you *could*. Film these ads in Central Park, I mean."

"You believe the National Weather Service?"

"I believe my bad knee."

Chance took the opportunity to snag Julia by the elbow and steer her around the corner out of sight. After kissing her—a much simpler proposition, now that her glasses had been replaced by contacts . . . and he was going to get used to the change without too much difficulty—he pulled back enough to prop his forehead against hers and whisper, "Hi."

"Uh-huh," she replied, her lips still parted eagerly and her eyes slightly dazed.

"They been at this long?" he asked, cocking his head toward the waiting room to indicate Eric and Dom.

"Only the last ten years."

"*This* time," he amended.

"Since we got in the car back in the city. More than once, Casey and I wanted to make the driver stop and let us out. I get the feeling her offer to go outside to the drop-off entrance was as much to get away from them as it was to wait for the other car and have one last cigarette before the flight. Not that she and Dom are any better."

He stared at her, confused. Marika—or was it Anika?—was the model; Heather was the hairdresser; and Val was the makeup girl. So, who was . . . "Casey?"

"The production assistant?" Julia reminded him. "She was at Geoff's last week?"

"The one with the clipboard? She do anything besides smoke and yell?"

"That's her job. Yelling, I mean. She's very good at it, too. Except she probably should have yelled a little louder at the driver to let us out. It wouldn't have been *that* tight of a fit, putting the two of us in the other car with the model, the hairdresser and the makeup girl. God knows, the model doesn't take up much room, unless you count legs."

"Just a cozy little weekend in the woods with half a dozen of our closest friends, huh?"

"More like eight, once everybody gets there," she corrected him with a wry smile. "Geoff and Damian'll be coming up Friday."

"Isn't that an awful lot of people to squeeze in one little cabin?"

"This is Hutchinson's cousin's cabin, remember?"

"The one with the villa in Grenada?"

"The same one." She smiled complacently. "And *we* call it a villa, but *he* calls it his 'cottage.' Having seen it, I'm almost afraid to guess what he considers a 'cabin.'"

"DEAR GOD." Casey's voice was uncharacteristically hushed as she breathed the words, almost devoutly.

"Who said that's a cabin?" Chance asked, equally astonished at the sight. "Marie Antoinette?"

"It *is* made out of logs, isn't it?" Julia pointed out, as if that could account for the understated description.

"Thousands and thousands of them," Dom contributed.

And to think he'd worried about finding enough privacy to be alone with Julia, Chance told himself, staring up at Hutchinson's cousin's "cabin" from the back seat of the four-wheel-drive Scout that had brought them from the tiny local airport they'd flown to after leaving Thunder Bay. They could get lost in there, if they gave it half a chance. He'd have to make sure they gave it their best shot.

Humble, it wasn't. While the bulk of timber-framing usually had a way of making structures look bigger than they really were, that didn't apply in this case. If anything, the building was so large, the massive logs hardly seemed bigger than sticks. He'd only ever seen one other building capable of doing that, the Old Faithful Inn in Yellowstone National Park. Though Hutchinson's cousin's "cabin" didn't have nearly that many rooms, he couldn't help remarking, "That's not a cabin, that's a lodge."

That impression was only magnified by the interior, he soon saw. What would have been a great room in any other timber-frame building literally *was* here; roughly the size of a gymnasium, it had a fieldstone fireplace spacious enough for them to roast a whole moose, if they were so inclined. Further distorting his sense of scale, the furniture and decorations were all typical of those in a normal-sized log cabin . . . except there were a lot more of them—and they looked a lot smaller—in here.

"So, what does somebody use a place like this for, anyway?" Chance asked, trying to take it all in with, at best, marginal success. "Boy Scout jamborees?"

"A weekend of hunting?" Julia suggested, eyeing a stuffed big-horn sheep—not a head, but the entire animal.

"He rents it to people like us for a major tax write-off," Dom guessed, starting up the broad staircase with his bags and a good portion of his equipment tucked under his arms, juggling the load with practiced ease.

"Dear God," Casey said again, digging a pack of cigarettes out of her purse with shaking hands.

Dom stopped long enough to glare at her disapprovingly. "Do you have to do that in here?"

"I should think you'd be able to avoid a little second-hand smoke in a room this size. And before you start griping again," she reminded him ominously, "remember that I'm the one in charge of room assignments, and you could find yourself *so* far upstairs, you'll think you're in training for climbing Mount Everest."

Besides silencing Dom, the announcement let Chance know whom he had to thank for putting Julia right down the hall. He didn't ask what made Casey do it—his guess was that Damian had said something about what he'd seen during the break at Geoff's studio—but, for that alone, he'd be willing to support her contention that the volume of air in the great room was more than sufficient to disperse all the smoke one person could produce.

And then once he discovered the connecting bath between the two rooms, he was ready to defend Casey's God-given right to do just about anything she liked. A woman whose sense of discretion was *that* highly refined was a woman whose good side he wanted to be on.

Several hours later, he started to wonder if both he and Casey had been mistaken. All the discretion in the world didn't do him a whole lot of good unless he and Julia did something they needed to be discreet *about*. So far, she hadn't given any indication that she'd noticed the connecting bathroom, not even when he'd left both doors ajar to take his shower. He would've been more than glad to skip dinner if he'd come out all squeaky-clean and found her waiting in his bed.

He hadn't, though. For that matter, she hadn't so much as called in to see if he was settling in okay. If he had to spend the next five nights trying to get some sleep at the same time as he was waiting for her to cross the threshold into his room, they were going to have to take him back home in a straitjacket.

He could easily imagine what that kind of scandal would do to Julia's precious campaign . . . and her big plans for her career. *Dentist-turned-model goes insane due to sexual frustration; swears the ad lady did it to him.* "A Current Affair" and "Hard Copy" would positively have a field day with the story, all plans for Ranger would have to be scrapped, the Fleischer brothers would go out of business, and she'd be lucky if she ever worked on Madison Avenue again, let alone started up her own agency.

That'd show her, all right...and never mind the fact that he'd be sitting in a hospital somewhere, weaving pretty baskets and asking if Napoleon was expected for dinner. If she'd changed her mind about what she wanted from him sometime between the time they'd gotten on the plane in Newark and when they'd pulled up to the cabin, the least she could have done was tell him.

In fact, Julia hadn't changed her mind; she was simply doing her best to be a bit more discreet about it. She'd already been much too obvious about her attraction to Chance, if Casey's room assignment was any indication...and she was sure it was. If the production assistant had figured it out that quickly, it was just a matter of time before the others did, too, and the advertising industry was far too insular for her to let gossip like that get started. By the end of the following week, their affair would be common knowledge all up and down Madison Avenue.

That awareness wasn't enough to change her mind, but it was enough to convince her to be more careful. Denise had been absolutely right—so, what else was new?—in her contention that what Julia needed to spice up her life was some good, old-fashioned fantasy, but she'd be damned if she was going to lose everything to get it. "No guts, no glory" didn't have to mean being stupid, after all.

All right, so she'd probably overreacted, going too far in the other direction in her quest not to seem too interested in Chance. For all intents and purposes, she'd been avoiding him ever since their arrival at the cabin— hiding out in her room when she knew that open door had been an invitation, and talking to other people all through dinner and then afterward, as though being

seen simply talking to him would fuel gossip—and it
was clear that he wasn't at all happy about it. What did
he want her to do, crawl on his lap in front of everyone
and stick her tongue in his ear? She'd be glad to do it
once they were alone, of course, but he'd just have to
wait until then.

Denise had never mentioned that indulging in a fantasy would be so stressful. They hadn't even done anything yet, and she was already on the verge of turning
into a basket case.

Not that there wasn't a certain thrill to it, too. At the
moment, she was the only one who knew about the
scandalously lacy black nightgown she'd brought with
her. Even Denise didn't know about it, despite her in-
spection of Julia's suitcase; she hadn't gotten that far
down before finding the box of condoms, and she'd
been having too much fun giving her grief to dig any
deeper after that. Julia intended for Chance to find out
about both of those things before he went to sleep that
night—if they ever went to sleep at all, that is. In a
good, X-rated fantasy, nobody ever needed sleep.

*But then, in a fantasy, nobody ever needed con-
doms, either.* And *that* was a point Julia would rather
not think about, because it brought the issue of fulfilling the fantasy of a lifetime with Chance Palladin much
too close to reality for her comfort.

By THE TIME Chance headed up to his room for the
night, he was mad enough at Julia to call her on it. She
hadn't said more than two words to him since their arrival at the cabin, and he'd had just about enough of it.
He'd had it even before Eric's little story about the relationship between sex and advertising, as demon-
strated by one of the senior partners at a major ad firm,

whose wife had cross-stitched him a sampler for the wall of his office that read "Get 'Em by the Gonads, and Their Hearts and Minds will Follow. Not to Mention Their Wallets."

Eric had seemed to think it was mighty funny, and so had everyone else. Everyone but him, that is. It would have been easy enough to attribute his inability to see the humor in it to the fact that he wasn't an industry insider like everybody else—as Casey had clearly done when she'd finally stopped laughing long enough to explain that it was often suggested that it ought to be the industry's official motto, the way Texans had "Remember the Alamo." He couldn't help wondering, though, if at least some of his discomfort was because it had raised the possibility that Julia had been applying that very principle to *him*.

Had she been leading him around by his glands, without the slightest intention of following through on it? Even worse, had he let her do it? He'd done everything she'd asked, agreed to every condition—even billboards and personal appearances, both of which had been against his better judgment. If that was what she'd been doing, it had worked like a charm. He hadn't merely let her get away with it, either; he couldn't have been any more eager to help her.

He could have sworn she'd wanted him, too; for that matter, he *had* sworn it, right after he'd peeled her off his body and put the lobster back in the sink. It had felt as if she really had. It just went to show how far wrong a man could be when he started thinking with the regions below his belt.

Thoroughly frustrated, Chance fought back the urge to slam the door to his room and told himself he had to calm down before he confronted her. He didn't want to give her the satisfaction of knowing she'd gotten to him. If he could just forget how much he'd wanted to give her satisfaction of an altogether different variety, forget what high hopes he'd had for this weekend, forget the way she'd felt with her legs wrapped around him, rubbing her heat against him while he'd had his mouth at her breast and . . .

"Chance?"

For a moment, he thought he'd imagined the soft, husky sound of her voice, but then he knew it was real. *Julia* was real—standing in the doorway to the bathroom, wearing a nightgown that might as well have been a cobweb for all the more of her body it concealed. Made of stretchy black lace that clung to her curves like a second skin, it was sheer enough for him to see the dark circles of her nipples through the fabric, as well as the darker triangle farther down her body, between where the gown nipped in at her narrow waist and its hem flared out to flutter around the tops of her smooth, pale thighs.

Every nasty thought he'd had about her manipulating him for her own purposes went out of his mind in that instant; in fact, so did every *thought*. She was so beautiful, so tempting . . . and she had her hair down. Just past her shoulders, it was curlier—and there was a lot more of it—than he'd ever guessed. He wanted to bury his face in its softness and breathe in her scent more than he wanted anything else in this world . . . except to bury *himself* in *her*, again and again, until they were both so utterly sated, neither of them could move anymore.

"Julia. . . ." he whispered, the word scarcely more than a sigh, as he stared at her, transfixed.

Smiling seductively, she stepped into the room, the movement of her hips making the lace skirt sway delicately back and forth around her thighs. As it did, he could see the last two digits of his phone number peeping out below the hem. So, she still had it, did she? It had been petty, God knew, branding her like a calf he was afraid might wander off, but it had taken some of the sting out of knowing she was out with Barth instead of him. At the time, his only motive had been to ensure that she wouldn't go to bed with him, too—something like that would be hard to miss and even harder to explain—but now, he found himself hoping there hadn't been one single second, either that night or since, that Julia had forgotten it was there.

After following the path of his eyes down to her thigh, she touched it with her fingertips, which then slipped under the hem of her nightgown, tracking the number he'd written on her leg up it almost to her hip. Chance couldn't say whether watching her touch herself did it—it could have been noticing the way her nipples puckered into tight peaks beneath the lacy fabric as she did—but he felt himself suddenly harden with arousal. At the same time, his mouth went dry as dust, and his heart pounded in his chest at a pace that would have been alarming if it hadn't been so exciting.

"Oh, God, Julia," he groaned, his hands closing into fists at his sides. "I'd started to wonder if you . . ."

"Changed my mind?" she completed for him, her smile now more seductive than gentle. "Didn't want you anymore? Just got cold feet?"

"All of the above, I guess."

"Try *none* of the above." She took several more steps toward him, bringing her close enough to lift her hand and run the tips of her fingers down the placket of his

shirt to his belt buckle. Bypassing it with a boldness that
made him shiver, she cupped her hand over his erection and said, "And I guess I don't have to ask if you still
want me, too."

6

JULIA HAD NEVER DONE anything so utterly brazen in her life, but then she'd never dared to give free rein to her most secret fantasies before, either. Just working up the nerve to do it had given her a certain amount of satisfaction, but that was nothing compared to the way she felt at seeing the gleam of appreciation in Chance's eyes. The knowledge that she'd inspired it made her feel more uninhibited, more powerful, more . . . aroused than she'd ever felt before in her life.

With one hand still cupped over the proof that he was every bit as aroused as she was herself, Julia stepped closer to Chance and lifted her other hand up to his nape. Weaving her fingers through the luxurious golden silk of his hair, she drew his head down and captured his mouth with her own. His lips were firm but yielding, beckoning her to do whatever she liked, and following her lead as she took him up on the offer. When she nipped at his bottom lip, they parted eagerly in invitation, and as her tongue slipped through the narrow opening, his met it in ardent greeting within.

His mouth was sweet, with a trace of the yeasty beer they'd been drinking downstairs, and he smelled of wood smoke from the fire, his woodsy cologne—definitely not *Ranger*—and the clean masculine scent that was his and his alone. As it engulfed her, inundating her senses, her fingers tightened reflexively to squeeze his denim-covered arousal. He groaned against her mouth, generating a shimmering vibration of desire that skittered across her breasts and downward to settle in the tender place between her thighs. With a groan of her own, Julia pressed her mound against the hard muscle of his leg and then demanded in a raspy whisper, "Hold me, Chance."

"I *am* holding you, darlin'."

"Tighter," she told him, her hand slipping around his body to the small of his back, where her fingers closed over his belt loop, gripping it as if it were a lifeline. "Don't let me fall."

"I won't," he promised, his arms tightening around her, even as she felt herself plunging forward.

"But . . ." she protested, too disoriented at first to realize that his solution for her weak knees began with making sure they were lying on a soft surface—namely, the bed. "*Oh.*"

Julia certainly had something to "oh" about. She was now sprawled atop Chance as he lay flat on his back, his hands on the backs of her thighs where they straddled his hips. Her nightgown was caught between them, the fabric wedged within the recesses of her body. As she reached to unsnap his shirt, his erection thrust up against her, rubbing the textured material over that exquisitely sensitive flesh.

While she'd meant to unfasten his shirt one snap at a time, tormenting him in between each with long, slow kisses, her plans evaporated as a rush of arousal coursed through her, making her shudder as her fingers clutched his shirt, yanking the snaps open all at once. Even after it was open to bare his chest, she wasn't able to caress him in the deliberately tantalizing manner she'd intended; she was too addled to do anything more than touch him with trembling fingers, as ragged breaths tore in and out of her chest.

Chance didn't have the slightest doubt about what had ended Julia's seductive efforts so abruptly. As he'd landed on the bed, he'd seen the way her nightgown was drawn tightly down her body, dragging it low on the upper curves of her breasts; once his eyes had followed it down to where it was tucked between her legs, it hadn't taken him very long to figure it out. As he'd seen her eyes glaze over, heard her struggle for breath, felt the moist heat of her body all the way through his jeans, he'd known a fleeting sense of envy that he, as a man, just wasn't capable of responding that intensely to something as subtle as a scrap of lace pressing against a single tiny knot of nerves and flesh.

What was even more reason for envy, though—to say nothing of anticipation—was knowing she wasn't done yet. His hands slid up from her thighs to her bottom, cupping the plump globes as he rocked her forward against him and pressed his mouth to the side of her throat. He knew the move rubbed the lace across that delicate kernel again, even before she cried out and her fingers twitched against his chest. Delighted, he boosted her farther up his body, lifted his head off the mattress, and touched his lips to the flushed skin above the neckline of her gown. Soon he was nuzzling his way across the mound of her breast toward its crest, still swathed—though just barely—in stretchy black lace.

When his tongue grazed the edge of her areola, she threw back her head and arched her back, and, finally relinquishing its tenuous hold on her nipples, the clingy material slithered down her breasts, baring them completely. Gazing at them, full enough to sway slightly as she moved, he couldn't imagine why he'd ever thought he was basically a leg man. If it had ever been true, it wasn't anymore. Legs, no matter how long or shapely, were just no substitute for the tempting roundness of breasts and bottom that epitomized femininity, and had since the dawn of man. And breasts had it all over legs when it came to sensitivity; he hadn't even touched them yet, and her nipples were already drawn into tight, hard peaks.

Taking one into his mouth, Chance finessed it, first with his tongue and then with the serrated edges of his teeth, as Julia wriggled over him, making sweet little noises of wordless demand. He'd wanted to come *with* her, *inside* her, the first time, but it was apparent that she was all but ready now. He was, too—or, at least, he would be, if he could just get her off his fly long enough to unzip it—but he didn't want it to be over that soon.

Setting aside his own wants and needs for the moment—and assuring himself that, in the long run, they'd both benefit from his self-denial—he followed the crease separating her bottom from her thigh as it curved down into that dark, mysterious cleft between her legs.

Lord, she *was* ready: so hot and wet, it drenched his fingers as soon as he touched her. He told her that in a hoarse whisper, his words explicit and erotic. Any worries he'd had that she'd consider them just plain dirty, instead, were instantly laid to rest as her breath caught in her throat, her eyes clenched shut, and the sultry rain of her desire flowed over his fingertips again. He eased one finger inside her, doing his best not to think about how good it would feel once it was his aching penis embedded so deeply inside her.

PLAY
ONE MILLION
BIG BUCKS
ONE MILLION
AND YOU COULD WIN THE
$1,000,000.00
PLUS JACKPOT!
YOUR PERSONAL GAME CARD INSIDE...
HARLEQUIN

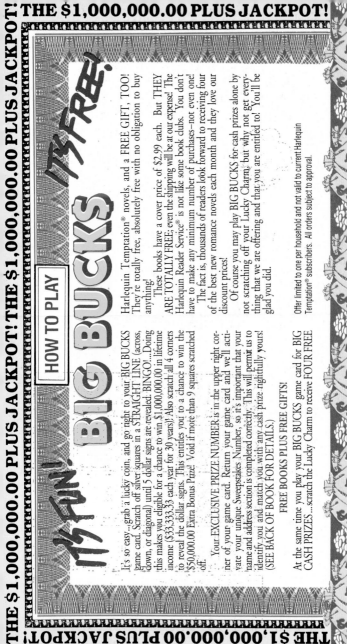

TWO WAYS TO WIN BIG BUCKS!

1. Uncover 5 $ signs in a row…BINGO! You're eligible to win the $1,000,000.00 SWEEPSTAKES!

2. Uncover 5 $ signs in a row AND uncover $ signs in all 4 corners…BINGO! You're also eligible for the $50,000.00 EXTRA BONUS PRIZE!

LUCKY CHARM GAME!

Claim
4 FREE books
AND a FREE
Mystery Gift!

YES! I have played my BIG BUCKS game card as instructed. Enter my Big Bucks Prize number in the MILLION DOLLAR Sweepstakes III and also enter me for the Extra Bonus Prize. When winners are selected, tell me if I've won. If the Lucky Charm is scratched off, I will also receive everything revealed, as explained on the back and on the opposite page.

142 CIH AOTJ
(U-H-T-08/94)

NAME _____

ADDRESS _____ APT. _____

CITY _____ STATE _____ ZIP _____

NO PURCHASE OR OBLIGATION NECESSARY TO ENTER SWEEPSTAKES.

© 1993 HARLEQUIN ENTERPRISES LTD.   PRINTED IN U.S.A.

HURRY!
This Jackpot
must be claimed!
Scratch
Here ⟶

EXCLUSIVE PRIZE # 6·0 156·072

BIG BUCKS

$

"Please, Chance...." The pitch and volume of her voice rose as Julia called his name; as gratified as he was to hear it, he was still sentient enough to recognize that everyone else in the place didn't need to hear it, too. Tipping his head back, he claimed her mouth, spearing his tongue inside as he moved his hand within her.

The noise she made then was still frantic but muted enough not to carry any farther than his ears. Hearing the demand in it, he slid his finger out of her and then back in, mimicking the motion with his tongue. Soon, he was stroking her over and over, faster and faster, the rhythm at her loins matched by the one in her mouth. She writhed above him, straining toward the release he was sure couldn't be too far away. How could it be? The only thing left was the climax—*climaxes*, he corrected himself, acknowledging the pressure in his own loins, which stridently reminded him that her release wasn't the end of this, by any means—and the eventual, gradual slide back down to earth.

"C'mon, darlin'," he urged softly, sliding a second finger inside her. "You're nearly there now, so just go on 'n' let it happen. You're so beautiful like this, I want to watch you...."

Suddenly jerking up her head and tearing her mouth away from his, Julia looked down at Chance, her eyes wide and unfocused as she gasped, "But you... We..."

"Next time," he assured her, ruthlessly pushing her onward, giving her no choice about holding back, as he knew she'd been doing, in order to wait for him. "Not until I get to see you...."

At last, he'd pushed her far enough, well beyond her ability—and her will—to delay the inevitable any longer. It began as her body went absolutely rigid atop his and her tight sheath closed around his finger like a fist . . . and, within a matter of seconds, with a low, keening cry, she was gripped by a series of spasms that managed to surpass anything he'd hoped to see.

"So beautiful. . . ." he whispered against her temple, damp with sweat, as he withdrew his fingers. He knew full well that he could have taken her higher still, coaxing one spectacular orgasm after another out of her until she was reduced to a blissful-but-thoroughly-exhausted state. He still had every intention of doing just that, but he was going to be with her all the way. As she breathed raggedly against his collarbone, he stroked her bare bottom, his touch soothing rather than stimulating as he gave her a chance to recoup. "So sweet. . . ."

When Julia finally worked up the strength to lift her head off his shoulder, she glared down at Chance through narrowed eyes and complained, "I was trying to seduce *you*, you idiot."

If she'd ever had the slightest illusion that the executive stare could still be at all convincing in the presence of the aftershocks that darted through her body, his grin shattered them completely. It was infuriatingly, superiorly masculine—or, to put it simply, smug. She distinctly remembered that he'd grinned at her exactly the same way right after he'd written his phone number on her leg. "I know, darlin'. I can't tell you how much I appreciate it."

Even more conclusively than the grin, the "darlin'" proved he hadn't believed her I-mean-business-and-no-mistake-about-it performance. "But I . . ."

"But you were headin' out of control like a well fire," he told her in that smooth drawl that had kept generations of Texan women complacent through tornados, stampedes, and generations of Texan men, "and I thought it might be a good idea to snuff it out before the whole field went up in flames. I wasn't shuttin' you down permanently, darlin'...just takin' some of the heat off and givin' y'all a chance to start over again."

"Huh?" *Whatever happened to plain English, anyway?*

"The way you were goin', y'all wanted it so badly, we'd've been done by now," he said bluntly. "Or at least *I* would've been—which pretty much amounts to the same thing."

Well, *that* was plain enough, she supposed. Accurate enough, too. Though she'd originally intended to take it slow and seduce the socks right off him, she'd practically ripped off his clothes when she'd gone careering out of control. "But I..."

"Trust me, darlin', you're not done yet, and neither am I." He moved his pelvis against her just enough to prove he knew what he was talking about, where both of them were concerned. "Not by a long shot. So, now, y'all just go back to what you were doin' before I interrupted you."

Removing his hands from her hips, Chance let them fall to his sides, showing Julia that he meant what he said. He'd only had the best of intentions, which hadn't had a thing to do with establishing who was in charge or thwarting her attempts to take the initiative. The only way his self-interests had been served by making sure he brought her to climax and left himself hard and unsatisfied was that he'd known they'd both be more satisfied if she proceeded with making love to him after the raging need that had been rushing her had been relieved.

Which it had.

Mimicking his drawl—and grin—as best she could, Julia told him, "And y'all just lie back and enjoy it."

"Don't y'all worry about that, darlin'," Chance assured her, stretching his arms over his head and hooking his hands together in a gesture of surrender. "Just take your time, because I fully intend to enjoy every last second of it."

Leaning forward, she braced her hands on either side of his head and touched her mouth gently to his, sipping at it as if it held the nectar of life. This time, there was no question that she'd be able to fulfill her fantasy of driving him to the brink with long, slow kisses and caresses and whatever else occurred to her along the way.

She leisurely explored every inch of his face with her lips and tongue, from the little scar near his hairline to his closed eyelids to the coarse stubble on his jaw. In due time, she found the sensitive rims of his ears and nibbled on them until he began to shiver beneath her. She savored the faint salty taste of the skin at his nape, the pounding pulse point in his throat, and the musky scent in the hollows above his collarbone until she began to shiver herself.

Moving to kneel beside him, she pushed the open front of his shirt aside, baring his chest for the same tender treatment. She blew gently on the patch of golden hair that graced the center of his chest, and ran her fingers through it as she took one of his nipples between her lips and felt it peak against the tip of her tongue. As she licked it, he cried out hoarsely, and his hands curled into fists above his head.

"Oh, God, Julia," he groaned as she slid one hand down his flat belly to his waist and skimmed it lightly along the top of his jeans. "Do you have any idea what you're doing to me?"

She guessed she did. His fly pressed insistently upward, leaving her with no doubt of the state of his body within. She moved her hand over the hard ridge, stroking him through the denim until he groaned again, and then undid his belt buckle, the button at his waistband and finally the zipper itself. Easing it down cautiously, she scarcely had it open before his brief-covered erection thrust out against her palm.

Sitting back on her heels, she pressed her hand against him and moved it slightly, caressing him through the white cotton and wondering if it felt as good to him as the lace against her most intimate flesh had felt to her. In a low whisper, she asked him, and then watched as he shuddered in reaction, his face tightening as if in pain.

"Not as good as your hands would feel touching me, darlin'," he forced out, his voice choked. "Oh, Julia...."

He dragged out the word as her hand slid inside his briefs and her fingers closed around him. His skin was so soft, and his erection so hard, she couldn't help but be fascinated by the dramatic contrast. Measuring his impressive size by touch alone, she slid her hand down to its base, and his hips suddenly bucked upward, pressing him more tightly into her hand.

In her rapt absorption with the effect she had on Chance, Julia didn't notice when he lowered his arms to his sides, one of his hands landing in her lap. The first she knew it was there was when he slid it up her belly under the hem of her nightgown, feathering his fingertips lightly across her as his thumb slid down her mound in order to renew its acquaintance with the still-engorged, newly aching bud hiding beneath it.

This time, however, she had no intention of letting him push her over the edge without him, the way he'd done before. Swiftly moving off the bed, out of his reach, she grasped the top of his jeans and peeled them off, getting as far as his knees before she remembered the obstacle of his boots. Crouching, she tugged them off and tossed them over her shoulder, hardly noticing the thud as they hit the floor behind her. By the time she was back to go to work on his jeans again, he was seated on the edge of the bed, his shirt already gone, watching her with eyes that glowed like barely banked embers.

Her eyes locked with his, Julia pulled his jeans the rest of the way off, reached for his briefs, then stopped long enough to press one hand to his chest in a silent request for him to lie back down. Once he did, she eased them off, dropping them behind her as her head dipped down toward his body. Her lips had barely grazed the taut, hair-roughened surface of his thigh, before she found herself dragged back up on the bed, lying flat on her back, with Chance's body covering hers.

"Sorry, darlin'," he whispered against her lips. "I thought I could let you, but...I'm so far gone now, the only handling I could take is for this."

Julia knew what *this* was, even before she looked down into her palm at the soft object he'd pressed into it. Of course, she had used condoms before; she'd simply never had any actual "hands-on" experience with them before. And, by all indications—including the expectant look that had been in his eyes just before hers had left them—he was counting on her handling it.

After staring at it for considerably longer than the object itself really warranted, she reluctantly lifted her

eyes to meet his waiting gaze. "I don't know how...."
she quietly admitted. "I never..."

While the eager gleam of arousal still glittered un-
abated in his eyes, it was joined by the softer light of
comprehension, and then understanding. Smiling
gently, he rolled onto his side next to her, covered her
hand with his, and squeezed it as he assured her, "That's
all right. I can teach you."

And he could. Though Julia had always thought that
putting on a condom was one of those embarrassing-
but-essential personal tasks best left to the person
whose body they were meant to fit, Chance had other
ideas on the subject. Turning it into an erotic adven-
ture, he encouraged her with soft sighs and words of
praise as she gradually gained the confidence to fondle
his body a good bit more than was strictly necessary to
get the job done. By the time she had it on him, he was
shaking as though he had a fever, and his breathing was
harsh and strained.

"Julia, darlin'...." He rolled on top of her, pinning
her to the mattress, as he began kissing her in a raven-
ous manner that suggested he never intended to stop.
While she certainly had no objections to that ambition, Julia braced her heels against the bed, bracketed
her knees around his hips, and pressed up against him,
demanding more.

Which was precisely what she got. As his body
slipped into hers, like a key fitting into a lock, it had a
similar effect on her, unlocking her responses, freeing
her senses to the prospect of sharing the ultimate pleasure with him. When he caught her heels and pulled her
legs up to wrap them around him, her body drew him
in more deeply, until she felt as if they were, in fact, two
halves of a whole. The impression was intensified by

the synchronized way they moved together, adopting a rhythm that steadily quickened as they hurtled toward their mutual goal.

With a sudden tremor and a high, wordless cry, Julia reached the point of no return a second before Chance did, but she didn't let that stop her. Knowing he was right behind her and gripping him so tightly that he had no choice except to follow, she let the waves of pure, blissful fulfillment engulf her as she cried out again . . . and again, as she was joined by his lower call of completion an instant later.

And then, Julia felt the earth shake, saw stars shatter and heard sky rockets in the night.

THE FOLLOWING MORNING, as Julia watched Chance gallop the big palomino stallion across the snow-covered field for the fifth—or was it the sixth?—time, she sighed with resignation when she heard Dom curse yet again. He was elevating profanity to an art form, getting steadily more creative as the morning wore on. So far, his outrageous, obscene and, occasionally, anatomically impossible injunctions had been directed at every member of the crew, including her, Chance, Marika, the snow, the horse, the cold, the lens filter, the wind, the entire nation of Canada, the sun, and somebody's—or some*thing's*—mother.

According to Eric, who was probably in the best position to know what he was talking about, Dom's real beef was with the sun and the snow. While the day before, when they'd arrived, there had been overcast skies that would have provided a natural filter for the sunlight, the clouds had all vanished since then, leaving pure white light that glittered on the snow so brightly, they had to squint just to see. The unblinking eye of the camera couldn't squint, however...or see, either, in Dom's expert opinion. Even before seeing the film, he'd told Eric it was going to look as if he'd taken close-up footage of a nuclear explosion.

Her sole consolation was that he wasn't blaming the problem on Chance's fair coloring...or the horse's, which she and Casey had picked because its coat matched Chance's hair.

Normally, Julia would have been able to work up a lot more energy to worry about it, but her energy level wasn't up to par, and neither was her concentration. She hadn't had much sleep the night before—not more than a couple of hours, and not all at once—but that wasn't why she'd been so listless and distracted all morning. That condition could only be blamed on her vividly disturbing memory of the earth shaking. Stars shattering. Those damned skyrockets in the night.

She'd always been convinced that such hyperbolic images were just romantic drivel dreamed up by people who were actually naive enough to imagine that fantasies were real, but at this point she wasn't exactly sure what she thought anymore. While part of her wanted to believe she'd experienced some significant, and magnificent, event that transcended mere fabulous sex, another part of her—undoubtedly the pragmatic part that had spent the last eight years spinning fantasies and calling them advertising—insisted she'd gotten snared in her own fantasy, lured in by the seductive appeal of fabulous sex.

Either way, she'd swear there'd been skyrockets. As surely as there were fireworks right now, of an entirely different kind.

This time, their source was Casey and Dom, both of whom were yelling at top volume, launching bursts of profanities and steam into the frigid air between them. As far as she could tell, the furious cameraman was accusing her of not coming prepared to deal with every possible contingency, including snow-blindness.

"Now, you just hold on a minute there," Casey snarled back. "If you check your contract—assuming you can read, of course, you silly jackass—it says *you're* responsible for all equipment needs, including those necessary to adapt to on-site conditions."

"And, if *you* check my contract, it also has an act-of-God clause covering unforeseen extreme conditions. And this damned glare . . ."

"It was talking about floods, earthquakes and hurricanes—not snow glare, which you should have foreseen . . . unless you were the only person who didn't know we were coming up here to Canada to find snow."

"And I suppose you knew there'd be snow glare bad enough to burn out the film."

"I'm not supposed to know that. That's not *my* job."

Behind her, Julia heard Eric sigh wearily. "God, I wish the two of them would go to bed and get it over with."

She turned her head to stare at him, gaping in astonishment. She couldn't have been any more surprised if he'd just told her Rachel was on the short list to win the Nobel prize for science. "Dom? And Casey?"

He sighed again, nodding so soberly she was forced to take him seriously, despite the implausibility of his claim. "They've been ripping slices off each other's hides through the last three jobs I've worked on with them. If they don't do it soon, they're both gonna bleed to death."

"But they hate each other," Julia protested.

"That's not hate," he pointed out. "That's sexual tension. But our schedule's too tight here for them to be figuring it out—or not—today. Whether it ends up with those two in bed or dead's just gonna have to wait for some other time."

His face set in an expression of grim determination, Eric stepped in to break it up. "Okay, that's enough."

Fortunately, he was authoritative—and tactful—enough to do it without bringing sexual tension into it. He was also authoritative enough to sound as if he'd spent the last several hours rethinking the schedule and everyone's duties, rather than as if he was flying by the seat of his pants. "If you can't get any decent footage with this glare, we're just freezing our buns off out here for no good reason. Dom, you get on the phone and see if you can catch Geoff before he leaves for the airport. If you tell him what you need, Damian can get it and they can bring it along when they come up. At this point, don't worry about the cost. Just get it if you think it might work."

Turning to Casey, he continued, "We're gonna do the interior stuff today, as soon as Dom gets off the phone. You've got the list of locations and props, so while he's calling New York, you work on the setups. Julia and Heather'll help, if you need it. Get Val to scrub Chance and Marika and make 'em up again for indoor shooting."

He looked around, making sure everyone had heard him and was ready to follow orders. "Got it? Let's go, then."

"Lord, that's impressive." Until Chance spoke, Julia hadn't realized he was beside her; how he'd gotten that close to her—and with the horse, no less—without her noticing, she couldn't begin to imagine. "If he'd been with y'all down in Grenada, you wouldn't've had to wait for the marines to save you."

"Our guess is, he was Hadrian in a previous life."

"Could be." He shrugged. "Looks to me like it'd probably be easier to drive elephants over the Alps than to make Dom and Casey stop fighting like a pair of cats in a bag. They like this all the time?"

"Eric says it's sexual tension."

Frowning, he considered the idea. "Could be . . . but if they don't do something about it pretty quick, somebody's gonna get hurt. If we're goin' in, I reckon we'd better put the horse back in the barn."

"You don't have to do that. You're the model, not the crew, remember?"

"Looks like Casey's got enough on her hands."

He was right. Casey was already halfway to the cabin, still arguing with Dom so heatedly that it was apparent she'd forgotten all about the horse. Which left . . .

"Give me the leash for that thing."

"The leash?" he echoed, clearly fighting back a smile. "You mean reins, don't you?"

"Whatever. It's a string, and it's attached to its collar."

"You mean bridle?"

"Whatever. I hold on to it, and the animal follows me."

"Like a big dog."

"A very big dog," Julia corrected him, warily eyeing it. Up close, it was even bigger than she'd thought, and it had an awful lot of very large, very nasty-looking teeth. Did horses bite, or did she only have to worry about it kicking her?

"We *could* just ride it back to the barn, you know."

"We?" She quickly shook her head. "I don't think so. I mean, I'm really glad to find out that you do know how to ride a horse, but I don't think . . ."

"That you want to get on it yourself?" Chance completed when her voice faded without finishing.

"Basically. It will just follow me back to the barn, won't it? I won't have to make it obey or anything, will I?"

"Julia, if you know this little about horses, I'm certainly not gonna hand 'im over and make you take him back by yourself." When she didn't answer, he frowned at her and asked, "Do you know how to take off the tack?"

"He stepped on a tack? Up here? In the snow?"

"Never mind," he muttered. "You just answered my question."

"Is he hurt?" He was only rented; how would she explain to his owner what had happened?

Shaking his head, Chance moved around to the side of the horse, and swung himself up into the saddle. He really *did* look like a cowboy, sitting tall in the saddle in his cowboy hat and sheepskin jacket. He just needed . . .

"Chaps," she said abruptly.

"Chaps?" he repeated blankly.

"Yeah. You know, those things that cover your legs." She moved her hands descriptively.

"I know what they are. I just don't know what brought them up, all of a sudden."

"We need to get you some," she pronounced with a decisive nod. "For the pictures."

"Julia, no one really wears chaps anymore, other than for rodeos. They're hot . . ."

"They're authentic . . ."

"... and heavy..."

"... and rugged-looking..."

"... and itchy...."

"... and women think they're really sexy."

He was silent for a moment, clearly baffled. "Sexy?"

She groped around for a delicate way to explain it, and was hard-pressed to come up with one—mainly because there *wasn't* one. At last, she admitted, "A lot of women seem to like the way they cover up everything but..."

"The butt and the crotch?" he offered with a grin, holding down his hand toward her. "With those convenient cutouts that frame both of them so nicely? And, may I ask, are y'all one of those depraved women?"

"I... You..." She wasn't at a loss for words on the issue of chaps anymore; other matters had taken its place in her mind. Such as, did Chance actually expect her to get up there with him? On the horse? All the way up there?

"C'mon up, and we'll talk about it."

He *did*. "Can't I just talk from down here? Look, you ride the horse back to the barn, and I'll walk alongside it...."

"Julia, gimme your hand, and I'll haul you up here." When she didn't move, he added, "I promise I'll hold on tight so you won't fall."

Her eyes shifted back and forth, between him and the horse, several more times, but she still didn't budge.

"C'mon up here, darlin', and tell me some more about those chaps you've got your heart set on."

Julia had been absolutely sure she wouldn't do it, but her hand reached up of its own traitorous accord. "Put your foot in the stirrup, then."

She did, and he pulled her up to sit in front of him. Even though his arms were wrapped around her, holding her there, she felt as if she were a million miles off the ground. She'd never realized horses were so *tall*.

"I like this way just fine, but you might feel more secure if you swing your leg over and straddle it."

If it meant moving that far off the ground, she didn't think she wanted any part of it, whether or not it might make her feel more secure afterward. On the way to doing it, she could fall on her head, and she had some legitimate doubts about just how much cushion the snow would provide.

"Maybe not," Chance finally decided, clicking his tongue and giving the horse a little kick in the ribs to signal it to start moving. By the second step, it was clear that Julia was looking for a handle, as if she were riding the subway and wanted a strap to hang on to. First she grabbed the saddle horn, but it swayed slightly with the horse's gait, and she immediately latched on to the horse's mane. Its withers shivered reflexively at her touch, as if shooing away flies, and with a funny little squeak, Julia let go and wrapped her fingers around Chance's lower arm.

He never would have guessed it. Julia, who was gutsy enough to make plans to start up her own agency by rustling clients away from her current boss—and who was, incidentally, obsessed with all things Western—was afraid of horses.

"C'mon, darlin'," he told her soothingly. "Just relax. I won't let you fall. I've got better plans for this body tonight than to be rubbin' in Ben Gay and puttin' hot compresses on it."

"What if it stampedes?"

"I believe you need more than one animal to classify it as a stampede."

"What if it bucks and throws us?"

"This horse hasn't bucked all day, even when Casey started yelling."

"What if . . . ?"

"Julia, we're at the barn already. You can open your eyes now and get down."

She reluctantly opened her eyes and then craned her neck to peer down at the ground, as if she were looking over the edge of the Grand Canyon.

"Unless y'all wanna spend the rest of your life sittin' up here on this horse, you're gonna have to take a shot at it sooner or later."

"I'm working up to it," she claimed.

"It's like getting into a cold swimming pool. You can dive in all at once and get it over with, or you can wade in slowly and stand there and shiver."

"I guess. . . ." Gripping the saddle horn and hooking her foot in the stirrup, she let herself down with more expediency than grace. Chance had to admit she looked happier with both feet on solid ground.

"I knew you could do it, darlin'," he told her as he swung down from the saddle and reached to put his arm around her waist. "All you had to do was make up your mind first, 'n' then it was no problem at all."

The instant his hand touched her back, Julia's head snapped up far enough for her to look over the back of the horse, and she stepped away from him, quickly breaking the contact.

"Julia?" he asked, bewildered by her sudden withdrawal until he followed her gaze, spotted the others slogging through the knee-deep snow toward the cabin and realized she'd been checking to see if anyone was looking their way.

"I can't, Chance. We can't."

"Can't or won't?"

"Can't," she repeated in a way that was starting to get on his nerves. When she used it like that, it always seemed "won't" was really what she meant.

Grasping her wrist in one hand and the reins in the other, Chance drew both Julia and the horse into the little barn. While it wasn't a whole lot warmer in there than outside, it was out of the biting wind—and out of view of the others on the crew. As if verifying his suspicion that Julia was all too willing to make wild, passionate, anything-goes love with him all night, *just as long as nobody found out,* she reached for him immediately, and it was the last he thought about anything for a good long time.

When he finally dragged his mouth away from hers, they were both flushed and breathless, and it took all the self-control he could muster up to tell her, "Julia, darlin', much as I'd like nothing better'n for the two of us to say the hell with the cold and finish this right here and now, we've gotta get back to work before they miss us and send out a search party."

And, as Chance finished settling the horse down in its stall and hurried to catch up with Julia, he found himself considering how quickly she'd gotten moving once he'd mentioned the threat of discovery...and wondering why it had seemed more threatening to her than, strictly speaking, made sense.

7

JULIA HADN'T FIGURED it could get any more complicated, but she'd been wrong. Why hadn't she remembered that one of the ads had called for Chance and Marika to be in bed? More important, why hadn't it occurred to her that Casey would pick Chance's bed to shoot it in? It was, after all, exactly what she and Denise had had in mind when they'd planned the ad: a piece of big raw pine furniture that would look right at home on a ranch, topped with a handmade quilt that looked as though it ought to be hanging in a museum, not covering a bed.

She'd nearly had heart failure when they'd walked into the great room of the cabin and Dom had casually looked up from his coffee and told them Casey was upstairs in Chance's room, making his bed. She hadn't dared to look at Chance to see his reaction. She hadn't dared to imagine what the bedroom looked like, either. They'd been in such a rush that morning, tidiness hadn't been a real priority, so all the evidence of the night's activities was still right where they'd left it . . . which, as she remembered, had been *everywhere*.

Oh, dear God. And Casey was in there now, so it was already too late. So much for any hope she'd had of keeping their little secret just between the two of them.

Though Julia could have used the moral support — and, since her legs felt awfully rubbery, maybe the physical sort as well — Val dragged Chance out into the kitchen to apply his new makeup, leaving her to face the music alone. At that point, she'd rather have faced a firing squad, but she tried not to look too panic-stricken or desperate as she headed up the stairs and down the hall to the closed door of Chance's room. After taking a deep breath and bracing herself for whatever might lie ahead—and, by then, she was beyond hoping it could be a turn for the better—she twisted the knob and pushed on the door.

And it didn't open. It didn't even budge. It was locked.

Locked?

Too addled to figure out the obvious—or to remember that she could go through her own room and the connecting bath to get inside—she tried again, with the same result. She was still jiggling the knob, still refusing to accept the fact that it wouldn't open, when she heard muttering inside the room, and then the sound of a familiarly smoke-husky voice. "Who is it?"

"Casey," she hissed through the door. "It's me . . . Julia. Let me in."

The key rattled in the lock, and the door opened just far enough for Casey to reach through and drag her inside. "It's about time you got here. I was running out of things to send Heather after to keep her outta here."

Julia supposed that, if somebody had to find out, she could be grateful it was Casey. No shocked looks, no recriminations, not even a raised eyebrow—merely orders to help her clean up this mess before everybody got up there and saw it.

"*You* had all the fun, so you have to help." Casey plucked a pair of white briefs off the floor and tossed them into an open drawer. As she pushed it shut, she said, "I'm still missing a sock, so if it turns up, this drawer's for dirty laundry. Nice nightgown, by the way. Where'd you get it?"

When Julia blinked at her speechlessly, unable to summon a lucid answer, Casey growled, "For God's sake, Julia, you can tell me. It's not like we'd have to worry about showing up somewhere looking like twins in matching outfits. Is that another one . . . there, next to the nightstand? How many *is* that, anyway?"

Julia groaned with mortification as Casey yanked the covers off the bed, sending several more pieces of foil drifting to the floor. Laying the quilt to one side, Casey balled the sheets up under one arm and tucked the pillows under the other. "I'm guessing this means the linen in *your* room is still clean. I'll be right back with it."

As she headed into the bath, Julia ducked her head under the bed, looking for any stray wrappers she might have overlooked. While she felt reasonably confident that she'd gotten them all, she hadn't found that missing sock yet. And, if she could miss something as big as a sock, it was a sure bet that she could miss something as small as a condom wrapper.

"You know, Julia, I was always sure you could do better than Barth. And I'd say Chance is definitely a big improvement on the boy wonder."

"Ouch!"

She hadn't known Casey was back until she'd spoken, and the sound of her voice—to say nothing of the editorial comment—had startled Julia into jerking up her head; unfortunately, it had still been under the bed at the time, and she'd rapped it on the solid pine bed frame.

"You okay there?"

She backed out on her hands and knees and then put her hand to the back of her head. It throbbed at the slightest touch, and she was sure she was going to have a goose egg by the following day. "Only if you consider a concussion okay—bearing in mind that the nearest hospital is only a hundred miles away. Did you *have* to mention B—*that* particular subject just then?"

"Sorry," Casey told Julia, wincing for her as she gingerly tested the injured place with her fingers. "Let's just forget I did, all right? If you won't mention *that* again—" she pointed at Julia's head "—I won't mention *him* again, either."

"It's a deal."

"YOU WANT ME to *what?*" Both the tone of Chance's voice and the expression on his face reflected an impressive mix of horror and embarrassment. Julia would have complimented him on it, but she had a feeling he wouldn't appreciate it.

She had a feeling he wasn't going to appreciate the attempt she was about to make to reason with him, either. "Now, Chance, you remember I said some of the ads'd be sexy, like the ones for Chanel and Calv—"

"You never said I'd have to take my clothes off," he flung back, his voice low but agitated. "Trust me, Julia, if you—or anyone else—had told me, 'And, by the way, you'll be bare-ass naked in some of the pictures,' it would've stuck in my mind."

"You won't be bare-ass naked," she pointed out. "Eric said it'd work out just fine if you kept on your shorts. You know, we were all hoping we wouldn't get to this point until later, once you were a little more comfortable in front of the camera. If it hadn't been for the snow glare, we wouldn't have . . ."

"I will never be comfortable enough in front of a camera not to mind having my picture taken in my un-

derwear . . . let alone having it be seen on national TV
and in every magazine printed in North America."

It would be a lousy time to remind him about the
billboards. And the posters. And . . . "But no one'll see
your underwear."

The green-and-gold flecks in his eyes glittered an-
grily as he glanced around the room, took note of the
fact that they had everyone's undivided attention, and
lowered his voice even more. "Can we talk about this
out in the hall? Just between the two of us?"

She didn't have a choice in the matter; he already had
her firmly by the upper arm and was heading for the
door, even before she had a chance to agree to step outside. He didn't stop until they were far enough down the
hall to be sure none of the others would hear them.

Leaning back against the wall and sighing wearily,
she tried again. "Chance, nobody's gonna see your butt
or your underwear."

"Damn right, they're not," he muttered, far enough
under his breath for her to be able to pretend she hadn't
heard it.

"If it's the ad itself you're worried about, you'll be
under the quilt. Marika's the one who's getting all the
exposure."

"So then, why do I need to take off my jeans at all?
Who'll know I'm still wearing them?"

"Anyone with eyes and half a brain. If you leave your
jeans on, there'll be too much bulk under the quilt for
it not to show. And in the TV ads . . ."

"In the TV ads?" he echoed unhappily, demonstrating that he hadn't missed the implication that there'd
be similar print ads, too. As if to be sure he'd gotten it
right, he asked, "Meaning, you expect me to do more
of these with Geoff?"

"There are corresponding print and TV versions for each of the ads," she admitted, though she'd wanted to break that news to him later, when he wasn't so worked up about it, "so that consumers can make the association between the two, and they can reinfor—"

"Don't bother explaining the finer strategies of advertising to me right now, Julia, because I'm in no mood to hear it. All I wanna do's keep my pants on."

"You can't."

There it was: that word again. If he never heard it again, that would be soon enough for him.

"Doesn't it bother you, Julia?"

"Knowing that women all over the continent'll be fantasizing about you in a bed, wearing nothing but a quilt?"

He didn't like her smile. It was too cheery, too enthusiastic, too...

"Chance, that's exactly what I was hoping for when I picked you."

He hadn't thought it was possible for him to get any more disturbed, but she'd just managed to send that sensation soaring to stratospheric new heights. Everything about what she'd just said set off a thousand alarms in his mind, but, at the moment, there were too many other distractions—primarily the issue of his seminudity—for him to figure out why.

"I know you don't want to hear about ad strategy right now, but that's what this is, Chance. All the other ads are teasers, and this one's the big payoff. Ultimately, selling fragrance is selling sex. There is no other point to after-shave and cologne. They're not a necessity, or even something you can buy and then flaunt as a status symbol—like, say, for instance, a Rolex. They're just a scent, and there's nothing more ephemeral or harder to define. If we're not giving them the scent itself—which we can't on TV, and I don't know anyone who isn't fed up with smelly mail and magazines anymore—we have to give them an image that's more than rugged and Western, or all they're gonna think of is the smell of sweat and a wet horse. We have to take them beyond that, create a fantasy world with a strong, handsome man and a beautiful woman...and, sooner or later, they have to end up in bed or there's no reason for anyone to buy the stuff."

His voice tight with irritation at the realization that she had a point—and a legitimate one, at that—Chance appealed to her one last time. "Just for a minute, Julia, try to separate the ad executive and the woman. Try *real* hard."

"I *am* separating it," she earnestly insisted.

"Try going with the woman this time, instead. If it doesn't bother you to think about all those other women fantasizing about me, doesn't the idea of me, all but butt-naked in bed with Marika for the rest of the afternoon, eat at you just a little?"

It was clear she hadn't thought about it that way...or, maybe, she'd been repressing it. Either way, he had her thinking about it now. If he couldn't get her to change her mind—and he was already half-resigned to the likelihood that *that* would be the end result of this discussion—he might be able to get some sort of admission out of her, at least.

But what sort?

Tamping down that doubt, Chance quietly demanded, "Isn't it gonna bother you to see me holding Marika in my arms, kissing her—you didn't think I heard anything Eric said once he told me to go in the

bathroom and strip down to my skivvies, did you?—
in the same bed we made love in last night?"

She swallowed heavily, and he repressed a smile,
knowing the ad executive wasn't doing the thinking
anymore.

"That's what I thought."

BY ALL APPEARANCES, Julia had gotten precisely what
she'd bargained for. After a few minutes in the bathroom—not even enough to make her wonder if he'd
changed his mind—Chance had emerged with a towel
around his waist, stridden across the room to the bed
and slipped beneath the covers, towel and all. When
Casey had stepped forward to take it, he'd been positively jolly, joking with her as he'd tugged it out from
under the quilt and handed it over. His relaxed con-
geniality had surpassed her most optimistic expectations when Marika, clad in his flannel shirt and roughly
six feet of bare legs, had clambered up onto the bed and
stretched out beside him atop the quilt. He'd followed
every last one of Eric's directions, right down to the
letter, with unfailing good humor. In sum, even though
he really wasn't a model or an actor, he'd done his
best—and a very good best, at that—to act like a professional in every way.

And, just like a pro, he'd gotten the job done. Dom
said the footage he'd gotten so far was fabulous: hot,
but not trashy; elegant, but not showy; romantic, but
not sloppy. The Fleischer brothers were going to be over
the moon when they saw it, and she was positive it was
going to get dozens of nominations for all the major industry awards. Starting up her own agency with that
kind of momentum behind her . . . Julia couldn't have
asked for any better beginning than that.

But if things had turned out so much better than she'd ever dared to hope, why was she so wretchedly miserable about it? She ought to be absolutely ecstatic. At the very least, she ought to be relieved. Just a few hours earlier, she'd been convinced they were going to end up with miles of unusable film showing Chance's best variations on looking stiff, uncomfortable, and embarrassed; instead, it looked as though he was genuinely having the time of his life, romping in bed with Marika as casually and naturally as if she belonged there.

In the same bed they'd made love in the night before, again and again, until she'd started to wonder if it was, in fact, a fantasy; according to everything she'd ever read, no man over the age of twenty-one could do it that many times in one night. What was he, some kind of sex machine?

It would certainly explain *this*. After all the bitching and moaning about how much he didn't want to do this ad, how could he look as if he was having such a good time now? What the hell had changed his mind so completely in the last hour and a half? Had he left his inhibitions in the bathroom with his pants?

Dammit, Dom and Eric were right. It did look great. Better than great; it was fabulous. It was going to look even better, too, once they edited the different angles together and added the music. Then it was going to be a real work of art, one of those legendary commercials remembered long after the product itself is history. Like the ads for the VW bug, showing it floating across the ocean. Or the ones for Short 'n Sassy shampoo, with Dorothy Hamill on ice skates. Or the ones for Dolly Madison cakes, with the *Peanuts* crew all on a sugar rush. All classics, each in its own way.

Assuming, of course, that the ads ever got finished. If she had to watch them go through this scene one more time—watch Chance run his fingers through Marika's hair, kiss her, kiss her again while he cupped her hip in his hand, and then shut his eyes and sigh while she nuzzled his jaw, smelled him and stroked his chest—just so Dom could shoot it from one more angle, they'd all better pray Casey was right about the holstered gun hanging from the bedpost, because she was going to find out whether or not it *was* just an incredibly realistic facsimile. If Casey was mistaken, Ranger would go down in history, all right . . . as the messiest ending to a campaign in advertising history.

"So why don't you go take a walk around the block?" Casey whispered beside her. "Go make coffee? Chop some wood? See if you can find the candles Heather looked for for forty minutes?"

"I'm fine," Julia answered tightly, wondering if her rancor was that obvious.

"Sure you are," Casey agreed sarcastically, confirming that it was. "Dom says he needs at least two more angles . . . which means at least six, because he thinks there's really a difference between film shot from a sixty-degree angle and film shot from sixty-two degrees."

"I know," Julia said with a sigh, understanding Dom's passion for the perfect. It could be a real nuisance, but it was why she'd hired him time after time. When all the irritation was over and she finally saw the commercial, there was always something wonderful enough to make all the headaches worthwhile.

"If you don't get out of here for a little bit, you're gonna turn into one of those homicidal maniacs in the workplace I keep hearing about, and I really don't care to know any more about the subject than I read in *Newsweek*. You've got that deranged, who-done-me-wrong look in your eyes already."

"If I make any sudden moves, hit the floor and stay there until it's over. I can promise I'll be aiming higher than that."

"Like at bed level?" Casey asked perceptively.

"Casey!" Dom bellowed, before Julia could answer. "What the hell is that shiny thing over there on the floor? Damn, I wonder how many other angles picked it up already that I didn't see."

As Casey hurried to remove the offending debris—no doubt about what it was—from Dom's precious frame, Julia decided it was an ideal time for her to make a tactical retreat...if, for no other reason, so she could have her giggling fit in privacy.

PRIVACY LASTED about five minutes, as it turned out—just enough time for her to get good and revved up, but not enough for her to reach the point where she'd start to taper down again. As a result, Julia was sitting in one of the big leather chairs in the great room, all by herself, giggling like a mental case, when Geoff and Damian walked in.

Just as Casey had done, they eyed her warily, as though they weren't sure whether or not she might be dangerous. Bobbing his head down to peer at her, Geoff ventured, "You okay, there, luv?"

There wasn't much she could say at that point. Explaining was impossible, and so was denial. At last, she managed to say, "I'll be fine."

It was close enough to the truth, since she didn't have to put a specific time estimate on it. *Eventually* would have been her best guess, anyway.

"Righto, then," Geoff replied, perfectly willing to accept that meager offering as adequate. "At first I thought maybe you had on the telly, but I see it's off."

"Was there something else funny I should know about?"

"I don't know if you'd call it funny or not, exactly. It all depends on your sense of humor, I guess."

Sobering with remarkable speed, Julia stared at him for a moment and then demanded, "Well?"

Clearly taken back by the sudden change, Geoff stared back. "Well, what?"

"We got one of the last planes out of Newark," Damian broke in excitedly, dumping his cargo from both shoulders with minimal care, especially since most of it was both fragile and expensive. "One of the last planes out of the whole mid-Atlantic seaboard, actually."

"They got the snowstorm?" Julia guessed.

"It's a blizzard, and they're already calling it the 'storm of the century,'" Damian announced. "We finally got to see a TV in Thunder Bay, and it's really awesome. High winds and snow as far down the coast as Atlanta. No telling when it's gonna stop, either."

"Word is, everything'll be shut down well into next week," Geoff contributed, with considerably less enthusiasm. "Roads, train stations . . ."

"Airports," Julia added, automatically filling in the gaps. "C'mon, Geoff, spit it out. What you're really trying to say is that we're stuck up here until they plow out the East Coast."

"I always said you were one smart lady."

It was really ironic. Beyond ironic, actually; ludicrous was closer to the mark. They'd come all the way to the wilds of northern Canada, looking for snow, and they could have had more of it than they'd know what to do with in their own backyard. The most ludicrous part of all was that the storm was everywhere but there, so they weren't snowed *in;* they were snowed *out.*

Once they'd figured out how to direct the big satellite dish outside in order to get news from the States, it confirmed Geoff and Damian's early reports. The entire East Coast was completely paralyzed, and it was still snowing, with no end in sight. Even the National Weather Service wasn't willing to hazard a guess as to when it might be over.

"D'you realize we could've gone down to Texas and shot these ads on location, with snow?" Eric observed a short time later, as they watched cars plow through three-foot snowdrifts—and into each other—in Dallas. When Damian had called up the news to the others, work had shut down for the day so they could all come down and see it for themselves. "What an opportunity... and we missed it."

"It's not like we could have known it," Julia consoled him. "And by the time there was enough snow in Texas to get excited about, we wouldn't have been able to get out of New York, so it wouldn't've mattered."

"Didn't I tell you they were right about this storm?" Dom demanded, looking as pleased as if he'd actually generated the storm himself. "If you didn't believe *them*, then you should've believed my knee...."

"If I hear about that damned knee one more time, I'm gonna cripple the other one," Casey threatened.

"But how'll I get back to New York?" Marika moaned. She was still wearing Chance's shirt and, maybe a pair of panties. Julia hadn't wanted to know for sure. Chance had pulled on a pair of jeans, but no shoes or shirt. "I've got a shoot first thing on Monday."

"Don't worry about it, luv," Geoff assured her. "Nobody'll be doin' anything on Monday...'cept, maybe, diggin' themselves out. It'll be like a holiday. A paid one for you, at that—on location, you get paid by the day, remember?"

Though Julia hated to think what this would do to Ranger's budget—Marika, Damian, Casey, Val and Heather were all being paid by the day—what could she do about it? She only hoped that since the Fleischer brothers were from Chicago, the city that invented harsh winters, they'd understand an extra expense that was due to snow.

Standing behind her, Chance smiled. Whether he was here or in Quakertown, it sounded as if his practice was going to be shut down for the better part of a week—he hadn't seen it yet, but, by all accounts, Quakertown turned into one giant skating rink in ugly weather—and he'd much rather be here in a cabin in Canada with Julia, all alone or not, than back in Quakertown all alone. With five days, maybe six, to work on her, he ought to be able to get Julia over this ridiculous notion that they had to keep their relationship a secret.

As far as he could tell, it wasn't much of a secret anymore, anyway. Even if anyone could have missed the fact that Julia had acted like a possessive—if not downright *possessed*—woman the whole time they'd been filming, Dom's incredibly undiplomatic reaction to that one shiny bit of condom wrapper on the floor had brought their secret out about as far as it could get without an official announcement. Given her attitude toward that subject, it was no wonder she'd gone flying out of the room as though her hair—tightly

wrapped, as usual, in some sort of twisty bun—were
on fire.

While he didn't share her conviction that their relationship ought to be a secret, he'd had a pretty good
idea how she'd felt; he'd felt his face burning with embarrassment, and he'd wanted to pull the covers up over
his head and hide. He might have done it, too, if Eric
hadn't cracked the whip and insisted on getting back to
work immediately after her departure.

Back to work and—for him—back to trying to figure out why Julia believed their relationship ought to
be a secret. All those hours of mindlessly following orders had given him a lot of time to think about it ... a
lot of time to remember things she'd said and done, put
them together a dozen different ways, and see if any of
them connected.

As it turned out, they did. They seemed to, anyway.

Whatever was happening between them—and, at
that point, Chance wasn't quite ready to decide exactly what it was, himself—it appeared to have shaken
Julia right down to her toes. He was sure her insistence
on trying to keep their affair a secret had less to do with
her worries about gossip than it did with her reluc-
tance to admit that it might be something more than a
fling. As long as nobody knew about it—or, at least,
as long as Julia could go on convincing herself that no
one knew—she could hang on to that illusion.

No commitments. No complications. No risks.

Considering that she practically made a career out
of taking risks in her professional life, he supposed it
was understandable that she'd want to avoid having to
deal with them in her personal life, too. Why else would
an exciting, vibrant, passionate woman like Julia have
spent the better part of the last two years taking the safe

route with Barth and convincing herself she was content with it?

Content wasn't the same thing as satisfied, however. Julia needed more excitement, more romance, than Barth could offer her. Chance didn't doubt that she would have figured it out sooner or later, whether or not he'd ever come onto the scene. As it was, she hadn't had to make that distinction; all she'd done was move from one safe route to another, apparently by adopting the tenet that he really was the Ranger Man.

By all indications, the entire Ranger campaign was based on Western fantasies Julia had harbored for years. He could see it in her eyes every time she talked about boots and hats, chaps and spurs, and cowboys and horses. He could see it in her eyes every time she looked at him, too. She did her best to ignore the fact that he was, in reality, a dentist, because admitting it, even to herself, would get in the way of her notion that he was her very own fantasy cowboy come to life.

Fortunately, he wanted Julia enough to give her exactly what she wanted.

THEY SPENT THE REST of the day fiddling with the satellite dish, watching live coverage of snow blanketing every city from Bangor, Maine, to Tallahassee, Florida, and laughing at the fact that they'd missed the "Snowstorm of the Century" because they'd gone to Canada looking for snow. Even though they didn't shoot another inch of film, and Julia could practically hear the meter ticking away the dollars like a stuck-in-traffic taxi, she wasn't worried about it, any more than she was worried about how long it might be before they could get back to the city. Being stranded up here in White Elk *did* have its merits, after all.

Since they wouldn't be going anywhere for a couple of extra days, they could take their time shooting the ads, a luxury they didn't ordinarily have when they were rushing to stay on schedule and keep the bean-counters happy. If Dom wanted to hang from the rafters and try a few takes from there—just to see if he came up with anything interesting—and Eric agreed, she and Casey wouldn't have to be the voices of reason in the darkness, nagging them about how that non-sense took time and cost money. Instead, they'd be free to let them give it a try... and then, later, tell the editor to lose the film on the cutting-room floor.

The cabin itself wasn't exactly a bad place to be stranded, either. While Hutchinson's cousin had learned his lesson, and the wine cellar was locked—though Dom swore he could take care of that minor obstacle, given time—there was a satellite dish, a big-screen TV and a VCR with all the latest movies. There was also a sauna and a hot tub. In short, it wasn't roughing it, any more than they'd been roughing it down in Grenada.

The most enticing benefit of all, of course, as far as Julia was concerned, was her temporary reprieve from the end of her interlude with Chance, when she'd have to head back to New York and send him back to Quak-ertown to fight the never-ending battle against tooth decay. She'd been dreading it—the end, that is, not tooth decay—even before they'd gotten out of bed that morning, thinking they only had three more nights to-gether. If they were lucky and the snow kept falling at its current rate, the entire Eastern Seaboard would be buried in snow up to its hips, giving them twice that many nights together before it was over.

Not over, Julia told herself, feeling a surge of hope rising up within her like a bubble...only to have it pop a moment later as she regretfully added, *But changed*. Who knew how long she'd go on feeling the earth shake, seeing stars shatter and hearing skyrockets in the night once the fantasy was back on plain, old, ordinary home ground and involved a two-hundred-mile drive?

But until then, she assured herself, stealthily snuggling closer to Chance on the sofa as they watched a group of confused Atlantans in spring jackets contending with gale-force winds and driving snow, she had five more nights...maybe six, if the snow fairies were on her side. And she intended to make every one of them count.

Which was why they slept in her room that night — when they finally slept, that is. Neither one of them wanted to waste the time on another "get rid of all the evidence and *quick*" clean-up of Chance's room. For that matter, Julia *wouldn't*; as soon as Casey announced that the first thing on the agenda for the next morning was to finish shooting *that* ad and then give Geoff a chance to take the stills, she made it quite clear to Chance that, if there was any more emergency housekeeping to be done, it would be his turn to do the honors this time.

He guessed he couldn't blame her for feeling that way. The room must have looked like a scene of an orgy before she and Casey had started. What he hadn't realized, however, was that making his room fit for public viewing had left hers looking even worse. Before they could go to sleep — or do anything else — they had to do something about the mess. Not real cleaning, of course — God knew, neither of them was the sort of neat freak who couldn't make love if there were any stray socks under the bed—but some things couldn't be ignored, like the lack of sheets and pillows on the bed.

"Looks like the key gnomes were busy in here," he observed wryly, eyeing the damage.

"Key gnomes?" she echoed, clearly confused.

"Key gnomes. You know, those little guys who come into your house at night, hide your keys, and generally mess up the place while you're asleep. Since you live alone, and you know that *you* certainly didn't make that mess or lose the keys...."

"...someone *else* had to have done it," Julia finished with a smile and a nod. "Well, *this* particular key gnome, I can identify."

"She chain-smoke and yell a lot?" he guessed, retrieving the ball of linen from the floor and dumping it on the bed. Assuring himself there had to be an end in there somewhere, he studied the lump for some indication as to where it might be.

"And she isn't the least bit slow about putting two and two together—or shy about revealing that the answer's four," Julia added, reaching for the wadded-up linen and finding an end with a speed and ease that made him feel like a dolt. "Fortunately, she does have enough sense to know when to keep her mouth shut."

Yanking the end, she deftly unreeled the linen and snagged the elastic edge of the fitted sheet. After sweeping the rest to the floor, he helped her stretch it over the mattress and decided that was good enough. Slipping his arm around her waist, he took her with him as he tumbled down onto the half-made bed and rolled her beneath him.

"But..." Julia protested halfheartedly. The dead giveaway that her objection had no real heat behind it was the heat in her eyes as they met his. They were like coffee—hot, rich, and so dark, they were almost black—but the jolt he felt as he gazed into them was far more potent than mere caffeine. It didn't just infiltrate his body, energizing it; it *transformed* it, in more ways than he could count. When Julia looked at him that way, he felt as though every nerve in his body suddenly took on a life of its own. Desires of its own. Needs....

He lifted his hand to the flushed surface of her cheek and caressed it. Soft, blush-warm...but not as soft nor as warm as her lips. He knew that, remembered it so clearly, the memory was enough to make him hard. As his fingertips followed the line of her jaw down to her mouth and traced the full curve of her bottom lip, it reminded him of how, the night before, Julia had tenderly stroked the swollen length of his manhood along the same path his fingers were taking now. When she let her lips part a bit, just enough to capture the tip of his finger, suck lightly on it, and touch it with her tongue, the evocative similarity was too strong for him to bear without shuddering.

As his loins tightened and he began to shake in response to that thought, Chance knew he was a goner. So was his resolution of fulfilling all Julia's fantasies— for now, at least—since doing it would require a great deal more self-control than he was capable of mustering up at that moment.

It was all he could do to manage enough thought to promise himself he'd try later.

8

SOMETIME LATER in the night, as Julia drifted in that groggy place between sleep and waking, she suddenly missed the warmth of Chance's body against her back. Vaguely unsettled at how rapidly she'd gotten so accustomed to the sensation that she was actually bothered by its absence, she reached out and slid her hand around beneath the covers, seeking him.

He wasn't there and the sheets were cool to her touch, revealing that he'd been gone considerably longer than it would take for a quick trip to the bathroom. Reluctantly letting go of the last vestiges of sleep, she forced her eyes open and squinted at the narrow beam of light that shone through the slightly ajar bathroom door.

What on earth could have driven him to crawl out of a nice, warm bed and leave her to go back to his own room at *this* hour? As far as she knew, she didn't snore—at least not badly enough to send him fleeing to another room for a little peace and quiet. She'd have been far more likely to pin the blame on her habit of stealing all the blankets, forcing him to go out searching for more...except for the fact that they'd been spooned together so snugly and cozily, he *had* to have been under the covers with her, no matter how greedy she'd been. So then, why was he gone?

"Chance?" Though she called out his name softly, the sound of her own voice seemed unnaturally loud and out of place in the dead-of-night silence.

So did the noise that carried back to her from the far side of the bath—a muffled, chinking sound she couldn't identify, beyond the fleeting—and wildly irrational—notion that it reminded her of loose change falling into a piggy bank.

"Chance?" she called out again, a little more loudly.

The metallic sound got louder, too, and Chance's long, dark shadow cut a sizable swath out of the lighted wedge on the bedroom floor. As he crossed the room, the shadow grew broader and longer, until, by the time he finally reached the doorway and came to a halt, it almost completely blocked the flow of light.

And no wonder, Julia reflected, gaping speechlessly at the sight. Despite the hour, when he should have been undressed, in bed, and sound asleep, Chance was fully clad, boots to hat. With the light at his back, he loomed in the doorway—now far bigger than life, at more than six and a half feet—his face hidden in the shadows, looking for all the world like a cattle rustler... or a stage coach robber... or, maybe, even a gunslinger. At any rate, something *dangerous*.

She shivered at the thought as he stood there, silently watching her stare up at him from the bed. She was positive that neither of them breathed; she would have heard it in the silence, which was even more absolute, now that he'd stopped moving. The only sound she could hear was the pounding of her heart, so loud she was sure he had to be able to hear it, too.

As if the impact of the moment wasn't great enough already to have Julia breaking into a cold sweat, she suddenly realized the odd sound she had heard and hadn't been able to identify—the sound she didn't hear anymore, in spite of the quiet—had been the loose jingle of ...

Spurs?

Oh, Lord. As Julia finally breathed, the air flowed out of her lungs in a long, ragged sigh that might have been an attempt to say his name. Though she barely understood it herself, it was clearly close enough for Chance to make it out, prompting him to step the rest of the way into the room.

My God, he really is wearing spurs, she told herself as the rhythmic cadence, still louder, commenced, ringing out with every step he took, as he got nearer and nearer, and then stopping when he did, just short of the foot of the bed. He looked down at her for an endless moment before he softly drawled, "Y'all trust me, don't you, Julia?"

A flurry of mingled confusion, apprehension and, above all, uncontrollable excitement skittered through her as she stared up at him, wide-eyed and tongue-tied. She didn't know exactly what he had in mind, but she did know that she trusted him, completely and unconditionally. At last, in a whisper that was trembly with longing and arousal, she replied, "Yes."

His hands closed tightly over the top rail of the footboard as he asked, "And y'all want this, don't you, Julia?"

Mesmerized by the arresting sight of the dull reflection of the light off the gun belt—and the gun—slung low on his lean hips, Julia shivered again. Did she want this?

"Oh, yes…" she breathed, eagerly scrambling to her knees in the center of the bed and reaching for him, oblivious to the sudden chill that surrounded her, raising goose bumps on her skin, as the blankets drifted down around her thighs.

Before she could make contact with him, he stepped back, out of reach, and she made a frustrated noise of protest; at that, he just shook his head and slowly smiled. "How's an outlaw supposed to ravish a woman if she ravishes him first?"

She didn't know how he knew; she didn't care. Returning his smile with a cunning one of her own, she promised, "Don't expect me to start screaming for help, though, because I might get it if I do."

"Darlin', I was countin' on you feelin' just that way about it." A beam of light—no more than enough to give her a quick, tantalizing glimpse of his face—slid under the brim of his hat as he cocked his chin at her, punctuating his instructions. "Go on, then. Get back under the covers, roll over on your side and shut your eyes again."

Once she did, the wait seemed interminable, and she couldn't keep herself from fidgeting with anticipation. Every tiny sound that broke the silence—and the feel of the mattress shifting under her as he moved onto the bed—only made the waiting more unbearable. At last, when she felt as if she wouldn't be able to stand one more second of waiting, she felt his hands press into the mattress on either side of her body, trapping her beneath the thick covers. Unable to lift her arms or roll onto her back, all she could do was tip her head to one side, exposing the hollow of her throat and hoping he'd take her up on the tacit offer.

And he did. His lips skimmed over the hammering pulse point just below her ear, making her heart beat even faster . . . and it beat faster still as he murmured in her ear, his words conjuring up dark, seductive images that were so eerily similar to her own fantasies, it was as if he'd read her mind.

"... Hiding up in the hills above the ranch, watching you—the rancher's beautiful daughter—for days without you knowing it ... Knowing I shouldn't, but doing it, anyway, because I can't stop myself.... Watching everything you do, just to see the way your body moves when you walk, the way the wind catches at your hair, blowing wisps all around your face.... Wanting to wrap its silk around my fingers, wanting to feel your mouth, sweet and warm, against mine, wanting to find out if your breasts'd fit in my hands as perfectly as I think they would...."

Julia wriggled restlessly beneath the covers—beneath *him*—utterly convinced that she was going to go out of her mind if Chance didn't touch her soon. Certainly, she was more than halfway there already, her breasts aching for his caress, and for the touch of his...

"Wondering how you'd taste if I peeled off your blouse and took your nipple in my mouth...."

Letting out a low groan at his vocalization of her thought, she arched her back so her breasts pressed against the top sheet, hoping it would do something to relieve the demanding pressure—or encourage him to move on—but, at the same time, knowing it wouldn't do either one.

"Wondering if you'd melt like butter in the sun if I slid my hand down your body...."

He wouldn't have to wonder anymore, if he'd just *touch* her, she wanted to cry. For that matter, he didn't even need to slide his hand down her body to make it happen, since she already was melting; she could feel the liquid heat flowing between her thighs as she reflexively squeezed them together.

"Wondering if you'd fly apart if I came into you, claiming you again and again...."

As her urge to turn her head to find his mouth with her own battled with her desire to let him continue to drive her mad with this slow, sweet torture, Julia started to tremble. She heard a sound that could only be a whimper, and knew it had to have come from her.

Fortunately, Chance heard it, too, and knew what it meant ... or seemed to know, anyway.

"Until one night, finally, when I can't stand it anymore ... your daddy's out on the range, so I know you're all alone in the house. It's dark, so I know you've already gone to bed. I sneak into the house, into your room, stand by your bed and watch you sleep. Of course, you wake up and see me there. You're a little afraid, but it excites you, too. You roll on your back to get a better look at me...." Shifting himself into an upright position atop her thighs, he nudged her shoulder, turning her on her back. Though the blanket was still pulled tightly across her body, it slipped down to her chest, baring her shoulders. "...And I can see you aren't wearing a nightgown."

"It's too hot," Julia whispered, as if in explanation, even though they both knew she'd fallen asleep, still nude, soon after they'd made love earlier.

"Maybe. Or maybe you knew I've been watching you all along, maybe you've been going to bed naked every night, lying there and waiting for me, hoping I'd come to you eventually...." He tugged the blanket down a bit, dragging the edge below her breasts, and she felt them swell even more as he looked down at them, his gaze as palpable as a caress. "Sure looks that way to me."

She shivered, and it wasn't from cold, as he unfastened the gun belt and dropped it over the side of the bed, letting it fall to the floor with a muted thud. His hat soundlessly followed it a moment later, and then she watched his hand move downward, past his hip to his heel, to . . .

She sucked in her breath so hard, he looked up in reaction to the sound, and then he smiled, looking like the living image of the dangerous outlaw he was merely pretending to be. "Well, I'll be damned. If I'd had any idea you were the kind of good girl who wants to be bad, I wouldn't've waited so long."

Never taking his eyes off her, Chance released the buckle on the spur, pulled it off the heel of his boot and held it loosely in his hand. She felt the uneven rise and fall of her chest as her breathing quickened, and he smiled again, as if that reaction told him everything he needed to know. Still holding the spur, he lifted his hand, brought it closer to her chest, and brushed one blunt, cold tip of the rowel lightly across her nipple. When she shuddered in response, he did it again, and then turned his hand to roll the edge of the wheel down her body.

Gasping and shivering again, Julia felt a row of goose bumps rising in its trail. Despite the implied danger of the act—*there must be* some *reason spurs make horses so angry,* she thought absently—his touch was so gentle and restrained, danger was the farthest thing from her mind.

"You like that, don't you, darlin'?" he purred, tracing the bottom curve of her ribs from her sternum down toward the bed.

"Mmm-hmm," she replied, totally incapable of words. At that moment, she couldn't even make up her mind whether she wanted her eyes open, so she could watch what he was doing, or shut, so she could feel it and just *imagine.* As they drifted closed for the third—

and, possibly, final—time, she felt him turning her, rolling her over onto her stomach, and her eyes flew open again, her body stiffening abruptly.

"There now, darlin', just relax." His voice was soft, his breath warm against her ear, and Julia could tell he was leaning over her, even before she felt the buttons on his shirt pressing into her back. "You're gonna like this, too. I promise."

His teeth closed over the rim of her ear, distracting her so that she didn't notice him moving off her until the rowel touched her nape and began to roll down her spine, his lips following it down her back, past her waist, to the cleft of her buttocks. As his mouth wandered over the round swell of her bottom, making her squirm with delight, she heard the same distinctly metallic sound that had baffled her earlier. This time, as aroused as she was, to the point where she was barely sentient, she identified it at once as the jingle of the spur; she even knew it was the sound of the spur falling to the floor to join the gun belt and hat.

Chance's hands gripped her hips and his teeth nipped at the fullest part of her bottom, revealing the tension that was rising in him, making it more and more difficult for him to maintain the pretense he'd put so much effort into creating. That strain was evident in every ragged breath he took, and in the thundering pulse at his temple as he rubbed his cheek against hers. When she twisted around to look at him, it simply confirmed that impression; the force of his passion—and his struggle to rein it in—had his face so tightly drawn, it looked as though he were in pain.

"Chance . . ." she whispered, reaching down to lace her fingers through his hair, push it back from his forehead, and caress the skin just below his hairline. A gust of air blew against her bottom as she watched him try so hard to suppress a shudder, it made her shudder herself. "Chance, I want . . ."

He lunged up to cover her body with his, and Julia felt the tremor rip through him, full force, against her back. One hand closed over her jaw, holding her head to one side as he found her mouth and plundered it with his tongue; the other delved downward between her thighs.

"God, Julia . . . ." he groaned, pressing against her, his weight holding her still without crushing her. "I want, too . . . ."

As his mouth closed over hers and he kissed her again, it made her head spin. She was only peripherally aware of his hand leaving her, the easing of his weight on her bottom, the groping at his clothing, and, finally, his hand sliding under her to tip her hips up toward him. It was only when he slipped inside her, filling her completely, that she touched solid ground, for a mere fraction of a second, before reeling off again.

"Oh, Chance . . . ." she gasped. "I can feel . . . I . . ."

At a loss for words, Julia gave up trying to find them. He was so deep inside her, deeper than ever, and she arched her back reflexively, drawing him in deeper still. He wasn't just inside her; he surrounded her, too—his legs bracketing hers and his arms wrapped around her.

"That's right, darlin'," Chance told her in a choked voice. "Feel it all. Feel how deep I . . ."

His next words—if there were any—were lost altogether, as he pulled back and thrust into her again. His fingers sifted through the thatch of hair on her mound, parted the folds of her body, and found the hidden bud there. When he touched it, she cried out as her body twitched with waves of pleasure; when he stroked it, matching the rhythm of his movement inside her, she felt her body tense all over, like a spring coiling within her, winding tighter and tighter, until she was sure she'd fly apart like a broken machine once it let loose. Surely, she couldn't withstand that kind of release, and come out of it intact.

When it came, Julia didn't simply fly apart; she *exploded*, with an impact that shook her right down to her curled toes and felt as if it went on forever. Forget skyrockets; this was *much* bigger stuff than that. And, just when she was positive it was over, it began all over again, as Chance's body tightened around—and within—hers, taking her with him, making them shatter together with an impact even more spectacular than before.

AFTERWARD, AS THEY LAY together, their spooned bodies spent and damp, Julia was filled with wonder at the fact that they were both still in one piece. She'd half-expected to find little bits of them scattered all over the room, like shards from a bomb, but it seemed she *could* withstand that kind of impact and come out of it intact. She just had as a matter of fact.

Her body, at least. Her soul was another story altogether. She'd never felt anything so powerful, so moving; she'd actually *cried*, she'd been so overwhelmed. She wasn't sure whether that sudden burst of tears had come as a greater shock to herself or to Chance; once she'd started gushing like a fountain, she hadn't been able to stop, and he'd been so upset, so certain he must have hurt her, he'd been stumbling all over himself, trying to comfort her. His earnest efforts had been so touching, they'd only made her cry more.

He'd been just as earnest—and far more understanding—once it was over, as swiftly and suddenly as
it had begun. While she'd been a bit embarrassed by her
behavior, he'd taken her into his arms, petted her gently and convinced her that, now that he knew what all
the crying was about, he thought it was, actually, kind
of sweet.

Almost as sweet, Julia thought with a tiny smile of
feminine triumph, cuddling back against him, as the
fact that he still had his clothes on. Though he'd started
out intending to create her fantasy, when it had come
down to the clinch, Chance had been so eager, so
aroused, so *wild*, himself, all he'd been able to manage
was his fly. It was a heady thought; she'd never before
made a man lose control of himself so completely, he
hadn't been able to wait long enough to undress.

All right, so she hadn't noticed it, either. He'd had her
so distracted, so excited, so *wild*, herself, by that point,
she'd been oblivious to the feel of denim against her legs
and bottom, and flannel against her back. Now,
though, running her toes down the front of his calf . . .

"Chance?" she murmured softly, certain, from the
slow rhythm of his breathing, that he was hovering on
the edge of sleep.

"Hmm?"

"Don't you think you might want to get undressed
before you fall asleep?"

"Too late," he mumbled, sounding as though it was
the gospel truth. In direct contradiction of that impression, he tightened his arms around her, nuzzled his
cheek into her hair and shifted his top leg farther over
hers . . . and, just as she'd gotten almost comfortable
enough to forget about pressing the point, she heard the
distinct sound of ripping cloth. "Damn."

"Damn, is right," she confirmed matter-of-factly. "That was a Pratesi sheet you just put your foot through."

"I just put that spur through," he wryly corrected her, shaking his head and swinging his legs over the side of the bed, and she heard the sound of still more tearing before he finally untangled his feet. "Pra . . . what?"

"Pratesi," she repeated. "Good linen. Roughly the price of a month's rent."

"Ouch." He reached to unfasten the spur, and then yanked the boots off, too. As he started on his belt buckle, he asked, almost in afterthought, "New York or Quakertown?"

Kneeling beside him on the mattress, she began to unbutton his shirt. "New York. Or four root canals with crowns, if that conversion's easier for you."

"Double ouch."

"Hutchinson's cousin'll still get off cheaper than when we raided his wine cellar."

"That's some consolation, I suppose." After she slipped the shirt from his shoulders, he lifted his backside up just enough to skim his jeans down his legs, but only got them as far as his knees before he paused. "Y'know, Julia, I was thinking . . ."

"Now, there's a dangerous notion."

His eyes skated sideways, meeting hers. "I don't know that you have a whole lot of room to talk, when it comes to that."

He had a point. If it hadn't been for her cowboy fantasies, he wouldn't have tried to enact one for her and ripped a hole in a sheet that cost as much as a decent used car.

"As I was saying . . . next Wednesday—not this one, but the one after we get back—Geoff's got another shoot scheduled, so I was thinking about coming into the city on Tuesday night, after we shut down the office. Maybe we could go out to dinner, or see a show...."

His voice faded off, and he studied her, frowning, just as she knew she was frowning herself.

"Something wrong? You don't want to go out? We could just build a fire and spend the evening at your place, if you want."

"What date is that?"

"Date?" he echoed, falling silent for a moment, apparently figuring it out in his head.

When he told her, she winced and shook her head. "I can't."

"Can't or won't?" he asked, his frown deepening.

"*Can't.* I . . . That's the night I'm going to see the new Andrew Lloyd Webber play with Barth."

HE MIGHT HAVE *ACTED* reasonable about it, but he hadn't been, Chance recalled the following day, as they set up for yet another take, from yet another angle, with yet another lighting scheme—this one courtesy of Eric, not Dom—of that blasted scene with Marika and himself in bed. At this rate, they were going to have to start making adjustments to hide gray hair on his chest by the time they were finished. Either that, or they were going to have to use a double for the close-ups.

This time, he had even more to keep his mind busy while he was waiting. The day before, when he hadn't been trying to work out Julia's insistence on secrecy and her fixation with Western fantasies, he'd been thinking about the night he and Julia had just spent in this very bed—hazardous territory, considering his attire . . . or, rather, his *lack* of it—but that subject had now been displaced by thoughts of Julia and *Barth*. Less likely to cause embarrassment, but just as hazardous, in its own way. He was every bit as apt to explode—just less apt to enjoy it.

"C'mon, Chance," Eric coaxed, for what had to be the dozenth time that day. "Would you quit the damned scowling and look like you wanna be there?"

"Y'know, there are plenty of men out there who would kill to be in your place," Dom added from behind his camera, which jerked suddenly as he yelped, "Ouch."

And women who would kill them for thinking it, Chance added silently. Apparently, Casey had just found some less-than-subtle way of letting him know that he'd better not be one of those men. It looked as though Eric had been right about Dom and Casey; if they didn't get to bed soon, there *was* going to be bloodshed.

He'd wanted to shed a little blood himself the night before, and he wasn't entirely sure whether he'd wanted it to be Julia's or Barth's. While the thought of removing Barth from the picture had had a certain primitive appeal, the truth was, Julia was the one who actually deserved it.

He'd tried to be rational about it, even though it wasn't a topic he was feeling particularly rational about. He'd reminded himself that she'd accepted the date with Barth before the two of them had even had dinner together. And then he'd reminded himself that Julia and Barth had been seeing each other for the better part of two years—a length of time that made it highly improbable that they hadn't been lovers, too.

"Smile now, Chance," Marika hissed, sliding her hand across his chest, with a look in her eyes that suggested he'd be missing a significant patch of chest hair if he didn't listen. "I'd like to get some clothes on again some time this century."

So would he. Lounging around all day in his Jockey shorts was getting mighty old mighty fast. He didn't find Julia's overt jealousy the least bit amusing anymore. For all that, he wasn't even sure he found it flattering anymore. Couldn't she see the inherent contradiction in it? Did she really believe it was all right for her to be possessive of him—when he was in bed with a woman she'd picked, and only because he was making the ads for her campaign—but balk at the idea that he might feel the same about her going out with a man she'd actually slept with? What did she think he was, anyway—made out of stone, an idiot, or just plumb crazy?

"Cut!" Eric yelled, sounding even more agitated than before. "Let's take ten, and try it again. Julia, you wanna see what you can do with Chance between now and then?"

"Excuse me?" she asked, her voice choked. Behind her, Casey tried to repress a laugh, and nearly succeeded.

"Look, I know he's not a professional . . ."

"Dentistry's a profession," Chance pointed out, even though Eric wasn't talking to him.

"In the business," Eric tightly amended. "And I know that working with virgins always takes ten times as long . . ."

Chance didn't dispute the point, but it did cross his mind. While he knew Eric meant a person working on his first ad—and he knew Julia knew it, too—she'd turned an intriguing shade of cherry red he'd never seen on her before, and he'd have liked to see more of it. He thought Casey might, too; she'd already given up altogether on her halfhearted struggle not to laugh.

". . . and you have to talk them through it, every step of the way," Eric continued, seemingly the only one there unaware of the unintended connotations of what he was saying. "Go on over there and start talking him through it, Julia, or we're never gonna get these ads done. *You* picked him, so *you* gotta make it work."

As Eric headed out of the room and the others trailed after him, Chance stayed right where he was. Not because Casey had forgotten to throw him a towel before she'd left—he'd already decided that being in an ad was a bit like being in the hospital, in that modesty ceased to be a real priority after the first day, but because, in this instance, being in bed and nearly naked might actually prove to be an advantage. Hadn't the entire Ranger campaign been based on Julia's favorite cowboy fantasies?

When she walked toward him, however, he felt that confidence begin to falter. Maybe being in bed and nearly naked wasn't such a good idea, after all. As mad as he was at her—and it pretty well pushed his temper to its limits—he still wanted her. He still wanted her a lot.

Oh, damn. At that instant, he would have given anything for a cold shower . . . or the cold steel of a real gun.

"I *heard* Eric," he told her tersely, before she had a chance to say a word. "Did y'all decide what you wanna do with me yet?"

Grimacing, she rubbed her fingertips into the tightly drawn furrow between her eyebrows. "That's not what he meant, and you know it."

"Do I?" he demanded, frowning at her. "I'm not sure I know what anything means anymore, Julia."

"Such as?"

"Such as how you can make love with me the way you do, and still not want anyone to know about us...."

"I..." Her voice broke after that single word.

"... or how you can look at me the way you do, and still not want to be with me instead of Barth."

"I..."

"Tell me how, Julia."

"I can't."

At Julia's answer, Chance's jaw tightened with irritation. He'd heard entirely too much of that word lately, and he hadn't failed to notice that whatever followed it had a nasty habit of being something he didn't like.

"Can't or won't?"

"Can't," she adamantly insisted. He was pleased to hear her sound every bit as unhappy about it as he felt, until he recalled that she usually did and it hadn't stopped her yet.

"Can't what?"

"Can't tell you... Can't explain... Can't expect anything, or get too..."

"And why the hell not?" he demanded, interrupting her before she could say "can't" again.

"Isn't that obvious? We don't have a thing in common. We live in different states, have different lives, different goals, different interests...." For a woman who claimed not to be able to explain, Julia had an awful lot to say.

But then, so did he. "Unlike you and Barth, of course, who have so much in common. The two of you have about as much active chemistry together as alcohol and water."

"And what does that mean?" she snapped.

"Structurally, they're so much alike, they can't generate a visible reaction. If you don't count the fact that they dry each other out, they're virtually inert. Is that what it's like when you make love with him? Or do you get as hot and wet for him as you do for me?"

She sucked in her breath so sharply, he knew it had to hurt, but he ruthlessly went on. If he'd been wrong about Julia and Barth, if they really were as happy together as two pigs in mud—though it was impossible for him to imagine how he could ever be that far wrong—he wanted to know it. Now.

"Do you rub up against him like a cat in heat? Make those hungry little noises all the way in the back of your throat? Go all to pieces when you come?"

"I . . ." The word was half gasp, half speech, but she didn't need to say it; he could see the answer in her eyes.

"I didn't think so." His voice dropped even lower. "If you did, you wouldn't've acted so damned shocked and surprised—and so pleased—when you did them for me."

"No . . ."

"Don't give me that bull, Julia. I *saw* it, *heard* it, *felt* it. . . ."

"No . . . I mean . . . I've never felt that way before, Chance, with anyone but you."

Neither had he. So much for her claim that they didn't have a thing in common. In their case, however, it generated one hell of a reaction. So then, why was she so damned and determined to hang on to the notion that all they could have was a fantasy? And why, in

God's name, was he considering letting her go on clinging to that premise? Had he lost his mind?

"Chance . . ."

As Julia lifted her head and met his eyes, the breath caught in Chance's throat. Mzzz Julia Adams, the woman who seemed to have made "no guts, no glory" a way of life, didn't have the guts to take the risks that really mattered. While she'd go way out on a limb for one of her campaigns, for a client, or for her career, she was so afraid to do it for herself—she couldn't without assuring herself she was only living out a fantasy and could run back to the security offered by Barth at any time.

Well then, what was he supposed to do now?

Let her.

He didn't know where the thought had come from, exactly. He did know that it didn't sound very smart. At the moment, however, it wasn't just his best option; it was his only option, as far as he could tell. If he confronted her with it, he had no doubts that she'd turn tail and run, as fast as her legs could carry her, and straight back to Barth. If he let it go on as it was, odds were, she'd have to figure it out eventually; she might be scared, but she wasn't stupid, after all.

But scared of what?

Until he figured that out, he was going to have to be as understanding as a saint, and as seductive as the devil...and go and get himself a good permanent pen— maybe a laundry marker—so she'd have an indelible incentive to keep her clothes on.

"Why didn't you, Chance?"

He almost reminded her that he'd done just that once already—and the fading evidence of it was still on her thigh—before he realized her question was about something else entirely. "Why didn't I what?"

"If you're this mad now...."

"No, I'm not," he told her, shaking his head. "Not anymore, anyway."

Julia eyed him warily, as if the assertion was too promising for her to believe. "Well, if you were that mad, why didn't you go back to your room last night to sleep?"

He'd considered it. Now, however, he was glad he'd decided against it, even if he had spent half the night turned away from her in bed, thinking about letting himself roll over and put his arms around her so he could get some sleep.

"And miss you nuzzling up against me most of the night?"

She turned as red as a stoplight, but he didn't stop. "Did I say I didn't like it? 'Cause I'd be lying if I did...and you know that as well as I do, I reckon, considering where your hands ended up, and all."

He hadn't thought it possible, but she turned an even more vivid shade of scarlet. Laughing, he leaned forward and dropped a quick, light kiss on her forehead...and then two more, one on each of her cheeks.

By the time Chance got to Julia's mouth, he wasn't laughing anymore. The kisses were slow and deep, and she was more flushed than ever, but not from embarrassment. Leaning back against the pillows propped up against the headboard, he hauled her atop his chest. Snuggling into him with a sigh, she skimmed the tips of her fingers along his collarbone, the heel of her hand brushing across his pectoral muscle just inches away from his nipple.

"That's it! That's it, exactly!" Eric shouted as he reentered the room.

As Chance groaned, his head dropped back and thunked against the headboard. He felt Julia groan, too, as she buried her face in the crook of his throat.

"Somebody...Casey, that's you...go on and get Geoff, right now," Eric ordered, clearly excited. "We've gotta let him have a shot at this, too, before he loses it."

"I don't think he's gonna have to worry about that any time soon," Casey muttered to Dom as she headed for the door.

Chance thought she was probably right.

9

"SO, HOW'D THINGS GO up in Canada?" Denise asked, tucking her legs up under her and wrapping her fingers around her coffee cup so tightly, Julia wondered if she was going to drink it or just hold on to it for warmth. During the week since the blizzard had buried Manhattan, the temperature had only risen a couple of degrees, sending their building's perpetually cranky boiler into shock. Julia's fireplace wasn't merely a pretty toy anymore; now, it was her major source of heat.

"You sure you don't want me to get you a stadium blanket?" Julia offered for the third time since Denise's arrival. "I've got the Giants and the Eagles and the Owls...."

"Couldn't make up your mind?"

"What was I gonna do, take the Eagles to Giant Stadium? I only wanted to see a football game, not a riot."

"To say nothing about getting killed once you started it."

"That, too. I'm giving you fair warning, this is positively your last chance. If you're gonna pick one, do it now, before I get settled." Julia knew she didn't sound very hospitable, but getting in and out of what was essentially a sleeping bag with sleeves was a major project.

"I don't need one, already. I've got long underwear, under my sweats...."

"Under the bathrobe?" Julia asked, pausing in her struggle to take a better look at her friend. She did appear bulkier than usual, now that she mentioned it.

"Right. If I put on anything else, I'm not gonna be able to move for the weight. Pass me the Cherry Garcia, and tell me all about Canada."

With a shiver, Julia held out the carton of ice cream, and Denise dipped in her spoon. If Ben & Jerry claimed ice cream would make them feel warmer, that was good enough for her; Julia was less than convinced that they were right. "They already had a nice layer of snow, just the way we wanted it, but they didn't get all *this*, and it wasn't as cold."

Tipping her head to one side, Denise narrowed her eyes at Julia. "If I'd wanted a weather report, I'd've turned on the TV and gotten it from Storm Field." For as long as Julia had known her, Denise had been fascinated by Channel 7's weatherman's name, investing countless hours in trying to make up her mind whether he'd changed it for the sake of his career or been given it at birth and was just fulfilling his destiny. "And, while we're on the subject of names and the men that suit them, how'd things go with Chance Palladin?"

"It's hard to say until we take a good look at it, but the extra time we had up there couldn't hurt. With as much footage as they shot—and as many rolls of stills—the law of averages says there'd be something decent in it, no matter what kind of idiots were behind the cameras. Being as it was Dom and Geoff, some of it's bound to be top-notch stuff."

With a put-upon sigh, Denise reached out and gripped Julia's forearm. "You're being evasive."

Julia didn't deny it. She couldn't; once again, Denise was right.

"I don't know why you keep forcing me to do this, but..." Denise paused just long enough to make the hair stand up on the back of Julia's neck, and her smile only enhanced the sensation. "So, what'd Chance think of the naughty little black nightie?"

By now, Julia should have known that lacy black nightgown couldn't have slipped past Denise unnoticed—or unremarked—no matter how far down in her suitcase she'd buried it. If she'd sewn it in the lining, Denise still would have found it—and mentioned it, too, sooner or later.

Julia was sure the hot blush sweeping up her cheeks said it all, even before Denise wryly observed, "I guess you don't need to answer that. Unless he's dead, he'd've loved it." Ignoring Julia's choked reaction, she took a dainty sip of her coffee and asked, "How'd the boy wonder take it when you broke the news?"

Ten seconds later, the mouthful of coffee was all over them both, as Julia continued to choke... and Denise continued to read answers into it so well, she choked, too. "You've been back in the city since yesterday, and you haven't told him yet? What're you savin' it for, girl—his birthday?"

"Since when are you so worried about Barth?" Julia finally sputtered, frowning with confusion. "You don't even *like* him."

"Likin' him's got nothing to do with it," Denise told her, frowning back, but with consternation. "I just can't believe you haven't told him you've met someone else."

"You make it sound like I'm making plans to run off with the milkman."

"The Ranger Man," Denise corrected her, setting down the cup before she had both of them—and the sofa and the rug—soaked with coffee. "What was it, then? A one-night? You can't really mean to tell me you're not gonna break up with Barth after this."

There were a lot of things Julia didn't mean to tell Denise, but she still always managed to find or figure them out. "We've got tickets for the new Andrew Lloyd Webber next Tuesday night."

"And, after that?"

"I . . ."

"Dear God, Julia! What is *wrong* with you?"

"Wrong?" Julia squawked. *"You're* the one who said there was nothing wrong with a little fantasy, remember? Whatever happened to all that stuff about 'getting the juices flowing and letting a woman know she's still alive'?"

"Did I ever say to get 'em flowing and then take 'em back to Barth? Uh-uh, girl. I don't think so." Pursing her lips, she shook her head. "Doesn't the idea of spending the rest of your life being bored into a coma with Barth make you wanna slit your wrists now and get it over with?"

"Not as much as the idea of . . ."

Before Julia could finish, the phone rang. Though she was reluctant to poke one hand out of the sleeve far enough to reach over the arm of the sofa, she liked that alternative much better than answering Denise, so she did it.

"Hello there, darlin'."

It was Chance. In a voice that was low with longing rather than for the sake of secrecy—God knew, there was no point in trying to hide a secret from Denise—she replied, "Hi."

"So how's it goin' up there?"

"I'm not gonna get to see any of the film or pictures until tomorrow, but they all keep telling me how great they look. Even Casey's impressed."

"Now, there's somethin'," he drawled, and she smiled at the sound, which was like an audible caress. "I get the feeling she isn't an easy woman to impress."

"You've got that right."

"Well, I wouldn't say you're much different."

"How tough can it be to impress a woman who's sitting in an apartment with no heat?" When Denise raised her eyebrows at her, challenging the statement, she admitted, "All right, so there is *some* heat. Denise is down here, sharing my fireplace and my ice cream and keeping me honest."

"If you wanna come down here for the weekend, I've got heat and a fireplace," he offered. "And I can get ice cream, too, if you tell me what flavor you like. As for keeping you honest...."

Julia smiled and sighed at the same time. "Do you have any idea how much work piled up while I was up in Canada? Even with the office being closed most of the time, everything's so backed up, I don't know how long it'll take me to get caught up."

"Probably until you get a real assistant," Chance observed. "What're you gonna do, work with your mittens on? C'mon down to my house and do it. I have all the comforts of home, including heat, which is one better'n your place. You could actually take a shower without runnin' the risk of frostbite."

"I..." It wasn't just the work, and she knew it. It was the thought of being in Quakertown for some reason other than to visit her parents. The dilemma of whether or not to call and let them know she was there; what to tell them, and what not to tell them; and how to keep them from jumping to the conclusion that she was ready to come back to Quakertown, settle down, get married, and give them some grandchildren—just like they'd always wanted her to do. The next thing she knew, they'd be sending out her résumé to every utility company and public agency in the county. Just what she needed—to have to explain to them once again why she wasn't interested in the security offered by working for either Ma Bell or Uncle Sam.

"Don't you dare say 'can't' to a man who just bought a pair of chaps," Chance threatened.

The noise Julia made was enough to have him laughing at her, and Denise staring.

"Leather ones."

She started laughing, too, while Denise continued to stare.

"I thought you'd appreciate it," he drawled.

"You did, did you?" All right, then. They could just stay in the whole weekend, and her parents would never have to know she'd been in town. "I'll be on the first bus out of the city after five o'clock."

"And I'll be waitin' at the bus stop. I'll be easy to find, darlin'. Just look for the only guy there in a pair of chaps."

CHANCE GOT TO THE office very early the next morning; after he'd hung up the phone, he'd been up most of the night. First he'd had to get his house whipped into shape for Julia's visit; there were probably still a few dust bunnies here and there, but at least he wouldn't be embarrassed by the state of the bathroom, and there were clean sheets on the bed. Once he was done, he'd been so wired, he hadn't been able to fall asleep for more than an hour or so at a time, until finally, just after five o'clock, afraid to risk it again, he'd gotten up, instead.

By the time Maggie got in, he'd washed out the coffeepot, made fresh coffee, and gone out for doughnuts. She'd appreciated the effort with the enthusiasm of a woman with a husband and two kids who all had very traditional attitudes about gender roles and household chores.

"You got some time to show Dave how the coffeepot works?" she asked, rifling through the doughnut box for the one with the most cream filling. "He thinks it cleans and refills itself, the same way the laundry gets done."

"Ooh...doughnuts," Amanda said with a sigh as she came in. Although the first patient wasn't due in for another half hour, she must not have had any domestic crises at her house, for a change, and had arrived on time. "Any special reason? I didn't miss your birthday, did I?"

Chance shook his head. "Not till July. I was running early and I just decided to stop and get them."

"Better get rid of 'em quick, before the patients start to come in," Maggie advised, licking powdered sugar off her fingers. "They're liable to get testy if they see stuff like that sitting around while you're lecturing them about too much sugar."

"I'll do all I can to help with that," Amanda assured them, reaching for a doughnut and the latest issue of *Cosmo*. Leafing through it, she stopped to look at the willow-thin model in one of the ads—and then at the doughnut in her hand—and let out an enormous sigh. "I might as well apply it directly to my butt rather than eat it."

"Tell me about it," Maggie agreed, nodding sympathetically as she tilted her head to one side to look at the magazine. "Is that what your ads are gonna look like, Chance?"

"No," he hastily insisted, after one quick glance at the ad. The black-and-white photograph showed a couple, obviously nude, embracing. While by no means explicit—his arm shielded her breast, and there was only the slightest hint of the curve of her bottom—it was indisputably erotic. It was also a mystery to him what the ad was for. "They want the ads to be sexy, but . . ."

"Sexy, huh?" Maggie teased.

"Yeah," he admitted uncomfortably. Smiling wryly, he shook his head. "Which means I take off my shirt. Julia'd describe it as, 'Sexy, but not too blatant.'"

"Huh?"

"Julia?"

He chose to answer the latter question from Amanda, since explaining Julia's pattern of double-talk was much too complicated. Half the time, figuring out what it meant was difficult enough. "Julia Adams, the woman running the campaign. . . ."

"Julia Adams?" Amanda echoed.

Maggie was no less surprised, even though she managed to say more. "Julia Adams from Quakertown? A year—two years, maybe?—older than me?"

His guess would have been that Maggie was older than Julia. Quite a bit older, to tell the truth. Marriage and two kids had certainly taken their toll, though the fact that she dressed and got her hair cut as if she were on the shady side of forty didn't help to make her look any younger. Unless she had another, older Julia Adams in mind. "I . . ."

"She'd be—what?—thirty-two now?"

Chance was grateful she'd taken the problem of guessing her age out of his hands before he'd insulted her.

"That's right," Amanda contributed. "She was a year behind me, but we were in the same algebra class."

And Amanda was only thirty-three? What did Quakertown do to the women, anyway—push them into premature middle age if they didn't get out of there in time?

"She was always really smart," Maggie said. "I remember her getting all those honors things in high school."

"So, Julia's working in advertising now? I heard that she graduated from college and got some fancy job up in New York—her mother and my gramma play bingo together at the fire hall—but that was all gramma understood," Amanda added.

He'd never realized Quakertown was quite that small. Maybe if he just let the two of them go on, he'd get to hear her whole life story... or what was left of it after Amanda's grandmother had gotten through editing out the parts she didn't understand.

"She isn't married yet, is she?" Amanda asked, sounding as if she thought Julia was beyond all hope of ever getting married, at the advanced age of thirty-two. Considering the way her own marriage had turned out, Chance wouldn't have expected her to be one of those types who thought everyone ought to be married with children and mortgages by the time they were old enough to drink.

He was less surprised that Maggie sounded much the same way as she shook her head and volunteered, "Well, she was always a lot more interested in studying and making a big success out of herself than she ever was in dating or parties. I always had the idea she'd wind up being one of those high-powered lawyers you see on the news all the time."

"I always had the idea she'd wind up doing anything that'd get her outta town."

So, that *was it.*

FOR THE FIRST TIME in longer than she could remember, Julia thought about calling in sick. Not that she was sick; she'd had her annual winter cold two months earlier—and hadn't called in sick then—so she was cold-proofed for the rest of the season. She simply felt like playing hooky. Doing a little unnecessary shopping. Treating herself to a nice, long, leisurely lunch.

And, while she was at it, temporarily avoiding Barth.

Damn Denise, anyway. Why'd she have to go and start asking questions that made Julia *think?* If she'd had doubts about what Julia was doing, couldn't she have kept them to herself?

Of course not, Julia told herself. *She wouldn't be Denise if she did.*

Terrific. If she had to have second thoughts, why couldn't she have had them first, when they might have served some useful purpose? At this point, it was too late for them to do much of anything but give her an ulcer.

Not that she regretted making love with Chance. It had been absolutely wonderful, beyond her wildest expectations. More than once during the week they'd been in Canada, she'd caught herself thinking that every woman should have the opportunity, just once in her life, to have her most cherished fantasy fulfilled . . . as long as she remembered it was only a fantasy, not real life. If she forgot that and let it make her dissatisfied with real life, she was liable to do something rash and irrevocable—like throw away a relationship that had been working just fine for the last two years.

And then, what would she have when the fantasy was over? An overstuffed portfolio, enough videotape to circle the planet and—if she knew the Fleischer brothers—a couple of cases of the worst-smelling men's cologne ever to be produced.

Maybe she'd better just forget shopping and lunch and go to work. The full extent of Rachel's screwups while she'd been out of town still wasn't clear, but she didn't doubt that there'd be at least one or two people she'd have to make peace with. If she was going to have any clients left to go with her when she left Locke, Reade and Hutchinson, she couldn't afford to let things—especially Rachel—slide until Monday.

And, while she was there, maybe she'd touch base with Barth, see if he wanted to go out to lunch, make sure they were still on for Tuesday.

Who said Denise always had to be right?

AN HOUR LATER, Julia settled back in Barth's "client" chair, took another sip of coffee and tried to decide whether he'd lost more hair in the last week, or if it only seemed that way because she'd forgotten that much was already gone. What had she been running her fingers through for the last two years?

Now, was that nice? she scolded herself. It wasn't his fault he was slowly but surely going bald. Like Denise had said, it was lousy genes. It wasn't even awful, nec-

essarily; contrary to the claims made in hair-replace-
ment infommercials, a man's hair—or lack of it—was
not the only thing women noticed.

They also noticed a nice smile. Broad shoulders.
Great buns. Hard thighs. Fabulous . . .

Oh, damn. So far, he was zero for six. At this rate,
she was going to have an awfully difficult time keeping
herself convinced that she was, in fact, perfectly satisfied.

" . . . Everybody says it's really fabulous," Barth continued, still talking about the Andrew Lloyd Webber
they had tickets for for the following Tuesday. "Ted and
Vanessa went last Saturday, and he was telling me it's
even better than . . ."

"Ted and Vanessa got back together? Since when?"

"Since he agreed to subclause 4B3."

"Oh." As if she was supposed to know what that
meant. She didn't have a clue, but she nodded, anyway, figuring she must not have been listening when
he'd explained it to her. And then she realized . . . "They
got back together, and you kept his tickets?"

Barth shook his head, frowning. Clearly, he understood her objection about as well as she understood
subclause 4B3. "He didn't ask for them, so I . . ."

"You didn't offer?"

"Once he told me he got two more tickets for last
weekend, I figured he didn't want them anymore.
Wouldn't you rather go on a Saturday night?"

"Only if I had an extra hundred bucks lying around
I didn't know what to do with," she pointed out. "He
probably bought the more expensive tickets because
they were all he could get at that point. It *is* the hottest
show in town."

"I hadn't thought of that." He shrugged. "Well, it's water under the bridge now."

Like a lot of other things, Julia reminded herself. Who was she, anyway, to be criticizing anyone else's questionable ethics? After all *she* was making plans to hustle her biggest accounts away from the agency.

But that's just business....

And what about Chance? That's just ...

"You wanna try that new Cajun place over in Soho tonight? I hear they're shipping live crawfish up from New Orleans, instead of making do with frozen, like everybody else."

Suddenly shaking, Julia struggled to her feet. "I ... can't. We don't ... have heat—well, not enough heat for anyone to call it heat, anyway, unless he has white fur and eats raw fish—so I'm going out of town ... down to Quakertown for the weekend."

She knew she was babbling, but she couldn't do a thing about it ... except hope he thought it was related to the coffee she was splashing all over his new Berber rug.

Trying to save it, Barth stood up, too, reached across the desk and wrapped his fingers around the mug. "Julia, you know how much you hate going back there, even if it's just to visit your parents."

He tried to take the mug from her, but her fingers tightened reflexively over the handle, gripping it so tenaciously, he would have needed the jaws of life to pry it loose.

"You don't have to go down there, you know. Why don't you come and stay with me until they get your heat f—"

As her arm jerked uncontrollably, his grip on the mug wasn't firm enough to prevent its contents from flying all over the rug.

"Oh, Julia. . . ." he said and sighed, looking down at the mess.

Julia let go of the mug as suddenly as though it were a live ember, leaving Barth holding it as she bolted for the door.

"Julia?" he called out to her when she was just inches away from making a clean—figuratively speaking— getaway.

Though it went against her better judgment, she stopped and turned back toward him. When she spoke, she thought she sounded surprisingly calm for a woman who was in turmoil.

"Thank you very much for the offer to stay with you, but I am going to Quakertown for the weekend. I have to go now. Send me the bill for cleaning the rug and I'll take care of it. And, by the way, I'm not . . . I can't . . ."

She stopped abruptly, and her lips pressed together as she stood there, frozen, wanting to say more and unable to. She felt as though she were standing on the edge of a high dive, trying to make up her mind whether or not she had the guts to jump.

"Don't worry about the rug, Julia," Barth said, before she could make a decision either way. "It's not important. What's bothering you *is*. Take the weekend at your parents' to think it through, and we'll talk about it on Tuesday."

"Tuesday?" she parroted, too confused to know what he meant.

"We're going to the theater, remember? Andrew Lloyd Webber? It's in your calendar in ink?"

Oh, God.

"If I'm back from Quakertown by then. I feel so . . . I might be getting the flu."

Which gave her the perfect excuse to take the rest of the day off. She played hooky. Did a little unnecessary shopping. And had a nice, long, leisurely lunch—by herself.

IT WASN'T WHAT she'd call her typical weekend in Quakertown. In fact, Julia found it incredibly easy to forget she was there. From the time she arrived Friday evening until she caught the bus back to New York on Sunday, they never left Chance's house. They didn't need to. Just as he'd promised, he had all the comforts of home, including working heat and a shower where they wouldn't have risked frostbite, if they'd gotten out of there before the hot water had run out.

And he hadn't been kidding when he'd said he bought a pair of chaps. While he hadn't actually worn them to the bus stop to pick her up—a wise decision, since neither of them would have been able to keep a straight face—he'd been wearing them when he'd come into the living room later that evening; which of them had enjoyed it more as she'd clarified exactly what it was about chaps that women found so sexy, it was tough to say. He'd never once complained about them being heavy, hot, or itchy.

She'd bought something, too, during her spontaneous shopping spree—and she had been wearing it when she'd gotten off the bus. Beneath her jeans and sweater had been a wickedly seductive teddy, little more than flimsy scraps of ivory silk held together by a few strategically placed yards of reembroidered lace. He'd appreciated it so much, it had been abandoned on the floor within minutes after they'd arrived at his house.

She'd appreciated his reaction so much, she'd forgotten about the chaps until they'd shown up later.

They didn't spend the entire weekend chasing each other back and forth between the bed and the shower, however. Julia had been telling the truth when she'd told Chance she had a lot of work to do. She'd spent the biggest part of Saturday afternoon curled up at one end of the sofa with the contents of her briefcase strewn all over the coffee table while he'd sprawled at the other end, reading for a while, and then dozing through an old World War II movie.

After they made supper and ate it in a kitchen that hadn't been remodeled since the days of harvest gold appliances, they built a fire in the fireplace, a project that made it all too clear to Julia as to why Chance had been so impressed with the gas jet in hers. When they finally had the damp, slightly green wood burning well enough that they thought it would make it on its own, they curled up on the sofa again, this time snuggling together at the same end. It was cozy and quiet, with only the sounds of wood popping and the sizzle of sap.

Slipping his arms around her and towing her back against his chest, Chance nuzzled behind her ear and whispered, "It's mighty nice havin' you here, darlin'."

Julia wriggled in tighter, distracting him so thoroughly, he scarcely noticed the slight hesitation before she answered, "It's nice being with you."

But she'd avoided saying "here," he noted, recalling what Amanda had said. "Here" was the place Julia least wanted to be. She'd worked hard to get out of here, and was still working hard to stay out of here. It was clear to him now that it was the driving force behind everything she did. Her zealous work on her campaigns, even if she had to overlook the fact that some of the products weren't just doomed to fail, but ridiculous. Her dress-for-success image, even if she had to suppress her femininity so far, the only trace of it that was left was lacy underwear. Her ambition to start her own agency, even if she had to heist her clients away from her current employer to do it.

And last but not least, as far as Chance was concerned, her relationship with Barth. She had to ignore the lack of passion—to say nothing of personality—because she was convinced she had to find a man who wanted all the same things she did, one who would never ask her to play it safe, sacrifice her ambitions...or move back to Quakertown, settle down, and start stagnating.

While he might. Or, at any rate, Julia thought he might, if she ever let her guard down enough to admit that her "cowboy" was really just a dentist from Quakertown...and that her greatest—or, at least, most elaborate—fantasy was, in fact, her notion that their affair was a fantasy.

Testing that theory—though he knew he was right—Chance casually asked, "D'you wanna call your folks while you're here?"

She shook her head, looking appalled at the thought. "They don't know I'm in town, and I'd just as soon keep it that way."

"So, that's why you didn't wanna leave the house, not even to go to the movies. I reckon they wouldn't be thrilled to find out their little girl's shacked up for the weekend with some guy, doin' Lord-only-knows-what," he teased. "Your daddy wouldn't be the type to come after me with a gun, would he?"

She didn't blush, as he'd expected her to. Actually, she was starting to look kind of green. "Worse than that. They'd want to have us over for Sunday dinner."

"C'mon, darlin'. Your mother can't be that bad a cook. You had to've learned it somewhere."

"I'm not talking about her cooking." He hadn't thought she was. "Chance, if they find out I'm here with you and we go over there for dinner, it'll just get their hopes up. Make them think we're . . ."

"Lovers?" he offered.

"Well, we *are*, but they'll get all these wild ideas. . . ."

"Like startin' to plan a wedding?"

If anything was wild, it was the look in her eyes. Deer in the headlights didn't look that panicked. It was even worse than he'd thought. "I . . ."

"We wouldn't want them doin' anything like that, now, would we?" Chance asked, doing his best to sound as if he thought the idea was absurd. He should have known better than to mention it at all; until she broke up with Barth, it was absurd. As he bit back a frustrated sigh and lowered his mouth to hers, closing the subject, he reminded himself that he'd never thought giving her the space to work things out herself and not putting pressure on her was going to be easy.

IT WAS WORSE than anything Chance had ever expected. He'd expected it to be unpleasant. Embarrassing. Even demoralizing. But he'd never imagined just how *painful* it would be. How could he? He'd never experienced anything like it before now, and his imagination just hadn't been capable of envisioning something so godawful on its own.

"Dear God, Julia . . ."

"Now, Chance," she countered. "You're just over-reacting."

He was not. In the last few weeks, he'd become very good at *under*reacting. Biting back his objections. Keeping his constant feelings of frustration tightly in check.

"But, you never said . . ."

"I most certainly *did*," she insisted. "Last week. And you said it was okay."

"You did? I did? When?" He pinned her eyes with his and, when hers skated away to the far corner, took an educated guess. "Last Tuesday night, when we were in bed, and I was half asleep?"

She pursed her lips, apparently thinking it over, before she reluctantly conceded, "That could have been when I mentioned it."

Which meant it had been.

"It's not as if there was anything you could do about it, anyway," she pointed out—not unkindly, just matter-of-factly. "It was gonna happen, whether you liked it or not."

He scowled, recognizing that she had a point.

"I really didn't *have* to tell you about the poster," Julia contended. "I could've just kept my mouth shut until you walked into Wanamaker's and saw it hanging there above the perfume bar."

He shuddered at the thought, turning his irritated glare on the dry-mounted poster, poised on an easel in one corner of her office. The instant he'd seen the photograph, he'd recognized that Geoff had taken it during that first session in his studio, just after Julia had slipped into the room. Instinctively aware of her presence, he'd peered into the darkness, looking for her—and Geoff had captured that moment.

And to think Geoff had yelled at him for moving. He had to have realized what he had, the second he'd taken it. Chance was still no expert on either photography or advertising, but even *he* could tell how utterly remarkable that photograph was. He hadn't realized Geoff was shooting at that moment—for that matter, he'd forgotten he was *there*—and it showed. The expression in his eyes was open and unguarded, revealing a haunting mixture of yearning, tenderness, and desire.

No matter how good it was, Chance wished to God they hadn't picked that one, though. Even though he'd merely had his shirt unbuttoned and hanging open, not off, and he'd had his jeans on, too, it made him feel more self-conscious—more naked—than he'd felt the first time he'd seen the finished commercial with him and Marika in bed. It didn't simply expose his body; it bared his thoughts, his emotions . . . revealing all the things he felt for Julia. He looked like a man in love.

Couldn't she see it, too?

Chance chafed at the knowledge that he couldn't object to that particular photograph for the same reason he couldn't raise any real objection to Julia continuing to see Barth; doing either one would mean telling her he loved her, and that was one thing he had no intention of doing until she took the first step. He still believed she had to want him—no, *love* him—enough to take the risk. Additionally, he'd had enough time to realize that he was going to have to make a lot of concessions to be with her, and it wouldn't be healthy for their relationship if he made all of them. All he'd gotten from her so far, though, were little ones—just enough to keep him hopeful.

Such as that, even though Barth had the advantage of being here when he was home in Pennsylvania, Julia had been seeing *him* more often. Or that she'd refused as many dates with Barth as she'd accepted. Or that she'd broken a date with Barth the week before, when he'd called at the last minute and said he could come up to the city, after all . . . while she'd never broken a date with him. Or, most promising, that Julia hadn't slept with Barth, not just since the first time they'd made love, but since the day they'd met. If she'd booted him out of her bed, it was just a matter of time before she booted him out of her life, too.

But for how long?

Tamping down his frustration with a skill he'd never wanted to learn, Chance resorted to the same means that had gotten him through this far. In a gentle reminder of what Julia would be missing if she didn't risk letting herself love him, he circled her desk, pulled her up out of her chair, sat down in it and pulled her back down onto his lap. Just before he kissed her with everything he could put into it, he told her, "Okay, Julia, I'm awake this time. You can keep the damn poster."

And she could look at it every day . . . until, sooner or later—hopefully sooner—she figured it out.

10

"DID YOU TRY the little tostadas yet?" Denise asked as she intently studied the ten perfect canapés she'd just meticulously arranged on her plate. By all appearances, she was deliberating which of them she could eat without doing irreparable damage to either the artistic balance of her composition or her figure.

Knowing better than to believe it, Chance did his best not to smile. It might look as though she was picking at the food as daintily as a bird, but he knew for a fact that it was at least her twelfth plate. Where Julia's friend put it all, he couldn't figure out. She ate like a roughneck just in off an oil rig, but she looked as though she hadn't seen a real meal in weeks.

"Or the little chicken-fried steaks?" she went on, ignoring his failure to answer her first question. "C'mon, Chance, help me out here. I feel like I'm talkin' to myself."

"Y'know, you can go on out there and mingle, if y'all want," he finally said. "Y'all don't have to baby-sit me, just because Julia's all tied up for a while."

"Oh, yes, I do," she contradicted him, selecting another tempting morsel of miniature Tex-Mex food from her plate. "I'm under strict, penalty-of-death-or-worse orders to keep tabs on you until she finishes and gets back. She's worried that you'll come to your senses and bolt back upstairs to your suite before the Fleischer brothers can get around to introducing you."

She might have a point; the thought had crossed his mind no less than a dozen times since their arrival a half hour earlier.

"And miss all the fun?" He could hear the sarcasm in his voice, and guessed she could, too. He'd decided the only thing that could be any worse than a cocktail party for a thousand or so people was one at which he was the center of attention—a live centerpiece, of sorts. "It shouldn't be much longer before the rodeo starts."

It wasn't entirely beyond the realm of possibility. Julia's party to launch the Ranger campaign had gotten just a little out of hand, to say the very least.

To her credit, it wasn't actually Julia's fault. Nathan Fleischer's favorite niece, Lisa, Ranger's director of public relations, had decided on the obvious Texan theme . . . and then followed through on it with a vengeance that suggested she must have been the pride of her sorority organizing theme parties back in college. It only began with the vast array of cocktail-party-sized versions of every indigenous Texan food from tacos to barbecue; there were also huge ice-packed tubs of Lone Star beer and pitchers of margaritas . . . and a real Texas line-dancing band. She'd wanted to get Willie Nelson, until Julia had told her—undoubtedly in that formidable, no-nonsense way of hers—that Willie wasn't in the budget.

Just about everything else was, apparently. It looked as though they'd cleaned out the entire state of Texas. There were enough yellow roses and bluebonnets to supply every beauty-pageant winner in the state through the end of the century, a huge Lone Star flag that had been raised above the state capitol building down in Austin on one wall, extensive collections of branding irons and barbed wire on the other two, and a mechanical bull, though no one had been brave—or crazy—enough to try it yet. There was even—though Chance couldn't imagine where Julia and Lisa had found one in New York—a live Texas longhorn penned up in one corner, and he'd heard rumors of an armadillo somewhere.

They'd had to pull the lavish spectacle off a lot sooner than expected, too. Julia had originally intended to give the party for the press, department store buyers, and other selected dignitaries sometime in May, two months before they broke Ranger to the general public. May would have given them plenty of time. Lisa, however, had discovered that April 21 was the anniversary of Sam Houston's defeat of Santa Anna at San Jacinto, which had ended the Texan War of Independence, liberated Texas from Mexico, and created the Republic of Texas; as far as she was concerned, that kind of coincidence was too good to waste.

Determined to make that date, they'd begun a frantic rush to get everything ready that still wasn't over; Julia had handed him over to Denise for safekeeping because she, Lisa and Rachel were all holed up in a conference room down the hall, stuffing little Ranger-logo shopping bags with party favors and press kits. By the end of the evening, half of New York would have videotapes of him and Marika in bed.

"You didn't mention that word to Julia, did you?" Denise asked, abandoning another empty plate and turning her attention to her margarita.

"Which word?" Watching the activity around him, he'd lost track of the conversation . . . again.

"*Rodeo*. Apparently, she and Lisa at least checked on the availability of Madison Square Garden."

"And that's where I picked it up. Julia told me that Lisa wouldn't drop the subject until she proved they couldn't afford Madison Square Garden." Chance sneezed again. He'd started to sneeze shortly after their arrival, and it hadn't let up since. "Until I moved up to Quakertown, I spent my whole life in Texas. How'd I never notice I was allergic to either roses or bluebonnets before now? For that matter, how'd I never notice how bad they smelled when they were put together? Maybe it's just that there's so many of 'em, all in one place?"

"Or maybe it's Ranger," Denise soberly suggested.

Chance began to laugh, and then stopped when he noticed she wasn't laughing, too.

"But the samples aren't here yet," he reasoned, his fingers tensing around the longneck bottle of beer as he gaped at Denise. "Julia's puttin' 'em in the bags right now, remember?"

"But the spritz ladies are," she pointed out. "They've been in here assaulting people for the last twenty minutes now."

"Denise . . ." he began, his voice measured and cautious. Low, too; he didn't think Julia would appreciate it if everyone in the room heard him ask ". . . Have you actually smelled Ranger yet?"

"Yes," she said noncommittally, just as quietly. "I have."

"And what would you say it smells like?"

She sniffed the air delicately, and then wrinkled her nose. "Eau de swamp. With something dead. And I'd say the body's been there at least two weeks."

He'd say it was an accurate assessment. "You're tellin' me this is Ranger? Does Julia know what this smells like?"

Denise nodded. "I believe she described it as 'essence of road kill.'" He believed it was equally apt. "How'd you manage to get this far into the campaign and never smell it?"

"There wasn't any reason to. We used empty bottles for all the shooting."

"Is it any wonder?" She nodded in appreciation of Julia's astute decision. "Julia was probably afraid one of 'em would get spilled, and Dom and Geoff'd never speak to her again."

"Could you blame them?" He took another sniff and wanted to sneeze again. "I don't think Julia has any reason to worry about Locke, Reade, *or* Hutchinson coming after her when she starts her own agency and takes Ranger."

"Because they won't want this smell in their office?"

He shook his head. "Because Ranger isn't gonna last long enough for her to take it."

"It'll make it through Christmas, even if it's on every half-off shelf in the country the day after," she said, sounding as though she knew what she was talking about. Probably because she did he assured himself. "That's long enough."

"Long enough for what?"

"For having the campaign seen." His confusion must have been evident, because she added, "Julia didn't create Ranger, so nobody'll hold that against her. She did the best she could with what she had to work with, and what she did is great. As long as people in the industry get to see the ads before Ranger bites the dust, that's what they'll remember."

"But...."

"She got nominated for awards for Sugar Tips, even after they went under." She shook her head. "Lousy product. Worse concept. But Julia made it work——for a while, anyway—as well as anyone possibly could."

"Sugar Tips?"

"The world's first—and hopefully last—intentionally edible fingernails," Chance heard Julia's voice say behind him, as her hand lightly touched his back just above his waist. She left it there, riding his waistband, as she looked at Denise and accused, "Some friend. Telling stories about me behind my back."

"I swear, Julia...I never mentioned that weekend you spent with the Bolivian Navy. Oops." Giving her a big grin, Denise held up her empty glass. "Now that you're here, I guess it's time for me to go find another margarita. And after that, I'm gonna go find out who *that* is."

Julia turned to look in the direction Denise indicated, and immediately knew who *that* was. "You know, he kinda looks like Wesley Snipes."

"I know."

She was gone in the next moment, and Julia noticed that she didn't bother making a detour for another drink on the way. In all likelihood, she hadn't wanted to give him sufficient time to escape before she got there.

"She didn't have to stay with me until you got here," Chance said. "I wouldn't't've run off. Honest."

She gave him a skeptical look. It was painfully apparent that he'd rather be almost anywhere else than there.

"How soon can we leave?" he asked, verifying that impression—as if it had actually needed verification. "Is this one of those put-in-an-appearance-early-and-make-sure-all-the-right-people-know-it parties you were tellin' me about?" His eyes darted around the room as he added, "If you just point 'em out, I can get it over with, and we can get outta here."

"That only works if you're a guest," she told him, earning a disgruntled frown. "If you're giving the party—which we are, in a way—you're stuck here until the bitter end."

"That's what I was afraid of," he grumbled. "And with all the free food and drinks, they're never gonna wanna go home. I get a hotel suite with a Jacuzzi, and I'm not even gonna get a chance to use it."

"Trust me, Chance, they'll leave soon enough. You'll get to use your Jacuzzi."

"I hope you mean *we'll*, darlin'," he said, his voice now low and seductive. "It wouldn't be the same all alone."

"You didn't look around your room very much, did you?" she purred. "I told the manager I had a bottle of champagne I wanted to drop off in your suite, and he let me in there this afternoon. I brought everything I need to get ready to go to work tomorrow, so I can stay the night."

His lips curved upward in a broad smile. "Now, there's an incentive to make it through this party, if ever I heard one."

"I think so," she agreed, returning his smile. It turned into a concerned frown when he sneezed. "Bless you. You're not getting a cold, are you? *Now*, after cold season's finally over? Tell me it's just allergies."

He winced and admitted, "Looks like they're to Ranger. Ask Denise—I've been sneezing my head off ever since we got here."

"Terrific." She studied his expression, trying to determine his overall reaction to Ranger. Other than the sneezing, of course. That didn't mean anything. Not really. "Are you gonna be able to wear it to personal appearances?"

"Are y'all gonna be able to sell any of that stuff is a better question," Chance corrected her.

"Why didn't you say something about it before now?" Julia demanded, not hearing his muttered remark as she worried about how to solve this unforeseen problem. Maybe she could fill him with antihistamines before every personal appearance. It would mean he'd be high as a kite at every one, but she didn't seem to have a lot of options. It wasn't as if sneezing was a voluntary response; it was a reflex. "Didn't you notice?"

"I didn't notice it before now because I'd never smelled it before."

"You mean, tonight's the first time you smelled it? But . . ." Julia stopped and thought about it for a moment. She had samples of Ranger both at her office and in her apartment. She'd let him smell it, hadn't she? "You didn't?"

"I didn't," he assured her. "Trust me, Julia, I'd remember it. The stuff really reeks."

She sighed wearily. "I know."

"No wonder y'all didn't want to send out scented cards in magazines. People wouldn't just be annoyed, they'd be callin' up the postal authorities and filin' complaints. Sendin' offensive material through the mail's a federal offense, y'know."

"I think they mean pornography," she pointed out.

"This stuff's a lot more offensive than any pornography I've ever seen."

Before he could elaborate on that claim—and before she could ask him to—a voice behind them heartily announced that their few minutes of privacy in the crowd were over.

"Such a nice party you and Lisa put together here, Julia." Even before she turned around, she knew who it was. There was no mistaking that accent for anyone but Nathan Fleischer. She hoped he hadn't heard anything they'd said before they'd known he was there; everything since Denise had left was either incriminating or embarrassing . . . or both. "Isn't it a nice party, Chance?"

Julia caught Chance's eye, trying to tell him the key word was *nice*. Nathan Fleischer was a genuinely decent man, and he didn't need to hear that Chance was chomping at the bit to get away from this party . . . or that he thought Ranger "reeked." It went without saying that he didn't need to hear Chance's plans for the Jacuzzi.

"Yes, sir, Mr. Fleischer," he answered politely, and she let out the breath she hadn't known she'd been holding.

"Nathan," he corrected Chance. "I have to tell you, I really like the ads you've been doing for us. You've never done this before, so they tell me?"

"That's right. I'm really a dentist."

"My sister Sylvia's oldest boy is a dentist, too. Out in Winetka. You wouldn't know him, would you?"

Confident that Chance was in good hands—and intended to behave himself for the moment, Julia murmured something about getting a drink and headed off to the bar, detouring along the way to stop at the buffet table. After she'd filled a tiny plate with an assortment of equally tiny foods, she started toward the bar, looked up, and nearly dropped her plate.

There, standing just inside the doors that led in from the hotel, was Barth.

The thoughts that ran through her mind in the next several seconds were disjointed, panicked and, for the most part, not particularly nice. To say she wasn't pleased to see Barth there would be an understatement of colossal proportions. To say she was completely surprised would be a lie. People from the agency stopped in at one another's parties all the time, for all sorts of reasons: to provide moral support, live bodies, or assistance, as the situation warranted; to get the free food and drinks; and to find out what their colleagues, who were actually their fiercest competition, were doing. Barth had come to parties she'd given before, and there were others from the agency there right now. While he hadn't mentioned he was coming—and she hadn't asked him—there was no reason for him not to be there.

No reason at all…except for the fact that I don't want him here.

For all the good that did her, Julia might as well not have wanted to be five-foot-eight, have hair that she needed a rake to control, or be as blind as a bat without her extended-wear contacts.

Julia knew the instant Barth spotted her, as he tipped his head in greeting and started across the room. Once she saw that he was headed her way, her eyes wandered over to where she'd left Chance chatting with Nathan Fleischer; she found him immediately, despite the throng. Though he'd convinced her he'd really rather wear a suit to this party and blend in than wear jeans and stand out in the crowd, he was still a standout, and it didn't have a thing to do with the extra height added by his boots.

Entirely of their own volition, her eyes darted back across the room to Barth, who had stopped to talk with the ad sales rep from *GQ*. Frowning, she observed that they could have been cast from the same mold, like a pair of slightly balding Ken dolls. Even the way they talked, with their attention straying all over the room as they made sure they didn't miss anyone more important—and not caring whether or not the person they were talking to at the time knew it—was the same.

On the other hand, she told herself, her gaze sliding back to Chance, he was giving Nathan Fleischer his complete attention, laughing at something he'd said and then saying something that made him laugh, too. Despite the fact that he didn't want to be at this party— or really, for that matter, want to be a party to this campaign—he was being very gracious about it, the same way he usually was. He had his occasional blow- ups, but they never lasted long, and he was a good sport about it afterward, whether he'd gotten his way or not.

Barth didn't blow up, she reminded herself, her eyes finding him again with some difficulty, now that he'd abandoned the *GQ* ad sales rep for a pair of perfume buyers from Bloomies. He argued, instead. No matter how well-reasoned his arguments—and they usually were, though there were times when he made no sense at all—they tended to degenerate into bickering and go on for too long . . . and he was hardly ever a good sport when he lost. He had enough trouble being a good winner; as a general rule, he was prone to gloat.

Still standing next to the buffet table, still holding the forgotten plate in her hand, Julia couldn't restrain her- self from letting her eyes—and thoughts—bounce back and forth between the two men, like furious volleying in a tennis match.

Barth or Chance. A perfectly good relationship that had been going on for nearly two years or love.

Love?

Love. That warmth she felt deep inside every time she was with Chance...or just talking to him on the phone. That despair she felt every time she thought about not seeing him again, once the Ranger campaign was over. That panic she felt every time she caught herself seriously wondering whether spending the rest of her life in Quakertown—or, for that matter, in any town that wasn't New York—would have to mean giving up all her most cherished goals. That incredible, all-consuming ecstasy she felt every time she felt the earth shake, saw stars shatter, and heard skyrockets in the night.

It wasn't just a physical release, either; she wouldn't have stayed with Barth this long if she'd never had an orgasm. It was different with Chance...flying all apart with such overwhelming force, and then feeling as though she was joined with him when it was over—not as two halves of a whole, but as though they were part of each other. Julia could now see that she'd recognized that difference—not just in the lovemaking, but in herself—that time she'd cried afterward. From that point on, there'd been no turning back.

There had, however, been a lot of standing still. All of it hers. She had to get it in gear and start moving forward... and she had to do it *right now.*

After setting her untouched plate down on the table, Julia wended her way through the crowd to where Barth was now talking to a man from the marketing team at Chanel. Without a pause in his discourse on the question of whether cosmetic advertising should focus on the product itself or on an image, he greeted her with a distracted smile that did little more than pay lip service to the word.

Well, at least she wouldn't break his heart, Julia mused. She didn't know how she could have been *this* stupid to settle for *this* little for *this* long.

"Barth..." she ventured at the first available silence, when he had to stop to breathe.

"Great party, Julia," he remarked. "Everybody that oughtta be here is. A little overdone on the Western stuff, but that's what happens when you get nailed down to a theme like this."

"Barth, could we go somewhere and talk?"

"Wanna go to dinner after this is over? We'll talk then."

She shook her head. "We *need* to talk *now*."

He stared at her; the curious look in his eyes told her that her adamant tone had caught him totally by surprise. The man from Chanel swiftly said goodbye and scurried off; the wary look in his eyes told her that Chanel wouldn't be calling her to work on a campaign for them any time soon. For once in her life, she didn't care.

"For God's sake, Julia, what'd you have to go and do that for? I had him all hooked and everything. All I had to do was reel him in, and you sure put a stop to that."

"So, give him another couple weeks to fatten up, like a good trout, and go after him again."

"Julia!" he gasped, clearly aghast at her flippant attitude.

"C'mon, Barth," Julia quietly suggested, refusing to allow herself to react to his reaction. "Let's go out to the bar and I'll buy you a drink."

"But the drinks in here are free."

He wasn't going to make this easy, was he? At this rate, it was going to be more trouble getting him somewhere where they could have a little privacy than it was going to be breaking up with him once they got there. If he kept it up much longer, she was liable to do something really petty and bitchy—like break up with him right here.

Oh, no, she wouldn't. Not in the middle of her party; the scene didn't bear thinking about. "But we need to find someplace quiet. We need to talk."

He stared at her for a moment as if he didn't know her, and then nodded. "Okay, Julia. You lead the way."

Well, there was a first. Telling herself that it was much too little—and much too late—for it to make any difference, Julia silently turned and led the way out of the room.

A HALF HOUR LATER, after the Fleischer brothers had stopped the music, hauled Chance up onto the bandstand, presented him to the horde, and finally released him, he was still wondering where Julia could have gone. More than that, he was starting to worry about it.

It was strange enough that, after all her efforts to ease him into this advertising stuff one step at a time, Julia had taken off for parts unknown just when he'd needed the most moral support. He hadn't wanted to get up there on that stage, in front of the thousand or so guests, and Julia had known that. It wouldn't have been nearly as much of an ordeal if she had been here, telling him that being the center of attention wouldn't be as bad as he thought and assuring him it'd soon be over.

What was absolutely unthinkable, though, was that Julia hadn't been here for what should have been her big moment of glory. She'd earned it; Lisa Fleischer's plans for this party had gone so far overboard, Julia deserved full credit for keeping it from turning into a real fiasco, which it could have done, all too easily. Besides that, now that he'd smelled Ranger, he was sure that this party—and that presentation—was going to be the high point of the entire Ranger experience.

According to Denise, Julia knew that, too. So, where was she, then? he asked himself, scowling darkly.

"You're looking very scary tonight," Denise remarked, coming up behind Chance so unobtrusively he hadn't known she was there until she spoke.

"That's probably because I'm *feeling* very scary tonight," he admitted. "I thought you were busy."

"I *am*," she told him with a singularly feminine smile, "but that doesn't mean we're attached at the hip. There are places I have to let him go alone."

"Oh," he replied, understanding and returning her smile with one of his own.

"You don't look so scary anymore."

A movement at the door drew his gaze in that direction, and his smile turned into a grin as he spotted Julia coming back into the room. "I don't *feel* so scary anymore, either."

"Where's she been?"

"I have no i—"

Before Chance could finish the word, Julia walked up to him, hooked her hand behind his neck and pulled his head down to give him a quick, hard kiss—right there in the middle of the Ranger party, in front of a thousand or so people.

When she let him go, stepped back and grinned up at him, he was speechless. He wouldn't have been any more shocked if she'd pulled all the pins out of her hair, stripped off her dress-for-success suit and the matching underwear with lace, and gone for a ride on the mechanical bull.

Denise wasn't speechless. "Well, I'll be damned. It's about time, girl. I was startin' to think I was gonna have to take drastic measures. For that matter, I was startin' to look forward to thumpin' you up side the head and knockin' some sense into you."

Julia just looked at her and laughed. He'd seen her laugh before—any number of times—but never like that. Usually, it had been at something funny. Now, however, she seemed to be laughing for the pure joy of hearing herself laugh. "Maybe you should've gone ahead and done it. A couple of weeks ago would've been a good time."

Chance just stared, still stunned. His eyes shifted back and forth between Julia and Denise, waiting for one of them to give him a clue as to what was going on.

"Can I save that permission for future use—like a Get Out of Jail Free card?" Denise asked.

Julia shook her head and laughed again. "Trust me. It isn't possible for me to be that much of an idiot, ever again."

"Julia?" Chance managed to say at last, and she turned toward him, smiling so broadly, she was positively radiant. It was that same beatific smile he'd seen so long ago at the grocery store, the one that had originally knocked the wind out of him. This time, however, it was generated by her sheer delight in seeing him.

The next thing he knew, he had her in his arms, holding her tightly and kissing her, loving her so much he was certain he'd burst with it. He'd never wanted her—and never wanted to tell her he loved her—more than he did at that moment. It wasn't just a want any-

more; it was a need that nearly made him chuck his vow
not to tell Julia he loved her until she broke up with
Barth. It took all the determination and self-control he
possessed just to show her, instead.

As she kissed him back, her arms raised to the back
of his neck, Julia marveled at the surge of love that
welled up within her. This was definitely more than
physical desire. It couldn't be contained—not that she
wanted to contain it—as it filled every part of her body
from her head to her toes, not just the obvious eroge-
nous zones. Somewhere in the back of her mind, she
knew where she was and knew how many people were
around them—she was sure she even heard applause—but she was too far gone to care; everything
else faded into insignificance next to Chance. Holding
him and being held by him, having him kiss her and
kissing him back, telling him . . .

Oh, damn.

Though she hated to do it, she forced herself to open
her eyes and wrench her mouth away from his, pulling
back far enough to look up at him. When he tightened
his arms, trying to draw her back against him, she slid
her hands down to his chest and pressed her palms flat
against it to hold that slight distance between them.

"Chance?" she asked, noting that his face was
flushed, his lips still parted and damp from their kiss,
his eyes hazy with arousal. After giving him a moment
to clear his head, she tried again. "C'mon, Chance, we
have to leave. *Now.*"

"Now? But you said that, since we were giving the
party, we had to stay until . . ."

"Just forget I ever said that. Denise'll cover for us. If
anybody asks, she can tell 'em you had a dental emergency."

"Just for the record, what kind of dental emergency would I have upstairs in my suite?"

"The armadillo has a toothache?"

"Armadillos don't have teeth," he pointed out.

"Oh." She smiled and shrugged. "I'm sure Denise'll think of something."

"So'm I, but I'm not so sure I wanna know what."

"Then, don't ask."

"Is that a good idea? If I'm gonna be publicly humiliated, I probably oughtta know the basic gist of it, at least."

"I told Barth I won't be going out with him anymore," Julia blurted out.

Clearly dumbfounded by the sudden announcement, Chance just stared at her, and she wondered if she should have eased into the subject a bit more gradually, the way she had with Barth. Well, maybe not *that* gradually; her efforts to be diplomatic about it had been so diplomatic, they'd merely confused him. It had taken him entirely too long to grasp the point that she wasn't too busy to have dinner with him that night, but intended to be otherwise inked-in for the rest of her life.

Thankfully, it didn't take Chance nearly as long to figure it out, and he recovered a couple of seconds later, grinning as his hands tightened on her waist. "What are we waiting around here for, then?"

"To make sure the applause is over?"

"I think they think it's part of the show."

"I'm sure they think it's part of the show."

"So then, darlin', let's really give 'em something to talk about."

Before Julia realized his intention, Chance swept her up in his arms and headed for the door, the crowd parting to clear the way for him as he waded into it.

Certain that a protest would be both pointless and senseless, she didn't say a word, but simply linked her arms behind his neck and held on . . . until she felt her shoe fall off.

"Chance, my shoe . . ." she cried, squirming around and trying to look for it, though she knew that was pointless, too. With all the flashes from the cameras, she couldn't see a thing except brightly colored spots.

"Don't worry about it!" he shouted back, so she'd be able to hear him over the applause that had broken out again.

"But it's Ferragamo! D'you know how much those shoes cost?"

"That's all right! Denise'll get it!" he assured her as he went through the door, which someone had jumped to hold open.

"Easy for you to say. It's not your shoe," Julia grumbled in a much softer tone of voice, once the doors had swung shut behind them, closing in the noise. "They can't see us anymore. You can put me down now."

"Not if I don't want to," Chance insisted, carrying her into the elevator and propping his shoulders against the back wall as he demanded, "Tell me again."

She blinked up at him, obviously confused. "Tell you what?"

"Barth?" he prompted.

"Oh!" she exclaimed before doing as he asked. "I broke up with him. Tonight. During the party."

So, that was where she'd been all that time. If he'd had to suffer alone, at least it had been for a good cause.

"I should've done it a long time ago," she admitted.

"Why didn't you, then?"

She shook her head and sighed. "It was easy—too easy. It was basically a relationship on automatic pilot, right from the start. It had everything I always thought I wanted, and I didn't have to work too hard at it. It's kinda funny, really. We should have been the perfect upscale couple, with everything in common, including matching his-and-hers goals."

"But?"

"But, like you said, we had too much in common. There just wasn't any chemistry there . . . or much of anything else, really. I tried to convince myself it wasn't important, even after I met you, when I should've known better. I . . . I love you, Chance."

And to think he'd only been waiting for her to take the risk of breaking up with Barth. He probably should have figured that once she'd taken that first step, she'd just keep going, beating him to the punch.

Which she had.

"I love you, too, darlin'. I've been in love with you since that week up in Canada."

"And just how long were you intending to keep that news to yourself?"

"Just until you caught up."

"From now on, I'll try a little harder to stay caught up, all right?"

It was a daunting prospect. Given her gung-ho approach to things, she'd probably leave him in the dust. Reminding himself that it was one of the things that had attracted him in the first place—as well as a key element of her success—he dropped a quick but tender kiss on her lips just as the elevator came to a halt and the door slid open. "Our floor. Rumor has it someone left a bottle of champagne in the suite."

"Do you believe everything you hear?"

"All depends on where I hear it," he told her, stepping out into the hall and heading for the suite. "In this case, I heard it from a very reliable source."

"Rumor also has it there's a Jacuzzi in there."

"And, in that case, I know it's true. I've seen it with my own two eyes."

"Good," she said, sighing, digging the card-key out of the pocket of his suit coat. "I'd sure hate to miss out on that Jacuzzi."

He nipped at her bottom lip in retaliation, and then kissed it to make up for it. "Now, *that's* chemistry."

"And you should know all about chemistry, Dr. Palladin."

Chance jerked his head back far enough to look down at her. "That's the first time you've ever called me that."

"I didn't fall in love with the cowboy, you know."

"You mean I bought chaps for no good reason?"

She smiled a secret feminine smile as she slid the card-key into the lock. "I wouldn't say for no good reason."

"So, you still think they're sexy?" he asked, pushing the door open with his back and carrying her inside the suite.

"Only on you," she assured him.

"We're even, then," he claimed. "You're the only woman I've ever thought was sexy in pinned-up hair and dress-for-success suits. That's because I know it's actually hell-gone-wild hair when you let it down, and you're wearin' matching underwear with lace under the suits."

"Am I?" Julia teased, running her fingertip along his jaw. "Maybe tonight, I'm not wearing any underwear at all."

Chance thought about the way he'd picked her up when he'd carried her out of the party, with her legs up in the air. He hadn't really been paying a lot of attention to whether her skirt was tucked up under her or hanging down in back. A thousand or so people, dozens of cameras . . .

"I guess I'll find out soon enough."

Epilogue

"LOOK, JULIA, it's not on half-off," Chance pointed out to her as they stood in the fragrance department of Macy's the day after Christmas. "Denise was wrong."

"It had to happen sooner or later, I suppose," she replied. "But then, so was I.... How could we have known Ranger's bad smell was just one unstable ingredient?"

"Two, actually." Which is what Ranger's product development labs had figured out within a matter of days after Ranger's introduction party, once Nathan Fleischer had asked what that godawful smell was, and somebody—Lisa, she thought—had told him the truth. "Either one of 'em would've been fine alone, but together..."

"Interesting chemical reaction."

"In this case, they didn't want a reaction, interesting or otherwise."

"At least it doesn't make you sneeze anymore. I was afraid I was gonna have to drug you for personal appearances."

"Thank God, they're over with now," he muttered.

"Are you telling me you didn't like autographing posters for all your fans?"

"Dentists aren't supposed to have fans, darlin'."

"I think you really liked all the fuss," she told him. "All this grumbling's just a smokescreen." When he leveled a distinctly dubious look at her, she added, "You signed on for another year, didn't you?"

"Only because I've got a vested interest in it now." Lacing his fingers through hers, he began playing with her ring. "What with me moving the practice up here from Quakertown and you going out on your own, we had to make sure we had some source of steady income, didn't we?"

Smiling at Chance, Julia raised her hand to touch his cheek. He really was one of a kind, she told herself; during all those weeks when she hadn't even been able to commit herself enough to break up with Barth, he'd been quietly checking out the possibility of moving his practice up to New York. By the time she'd finally been able to bring herself to consider moving down to Quakertown and starting her agency in Philadelphia, instead, he'd assured her that it really wasn't necessary, since he'd all but picked Quakertown at random to start with, and it wasn't as if he had any real ties there.

"We'll make it," she assured him. "You're getting more new patients practically every day, I've got a few accounts already, and Nathan Fleischer's made it quite clear that I was the reason he went with Locke, Reade and Hutchinson in the first place, so he's not interested in staying there once his contract's up."

"It didn't help matters any that they gave Ranger to Barth," he reminded her.

"It didn't help that they gave Rachel to Barth, either."

"That goes without saying. The kind of damage those two could do together..."

"*Have done,*" Julia corrected him. "Denise said that Nathan made such an uproar about Rachel's latest big mistake that Hutchinson wasn't too upset about him leaving, as long as he didn't sue."

"So, you didn't even have to hustle Ranger away. Barth and Rachel chased them off."

"Basically. Did I mention that Nathan called the other day, just to shoot the bull and run their next new line past me?"

"Even though you can't start working on it until their contract runs out at the end of next month?"

She nodded and grinned. "They're calling it 'Paladin.'"

"What?" Chance barked, a definite look of panic in his eyes.

"As in knight," Julia clarified. "The medieval kind. Armor and chargers, castles and dragons, chivalry and pageantry and all that good stuff. Sort of like the old British Sterling ads."

"I'm tellin' y'all right now, darlin'. I don't do armor, so don't go gettin' any ideas."

HARLEQUIN®

Temptation®

COMING NEXT MONTH

#505 EVEN COWBOYS GET THE BLUES Carin Rafferty
Lost Loves, Book 5

No *way* would Annie O'Neill ever work with her lying and cheating
ex-husband again. So what if Tanner Chapel needed her to help write
his country songs? So what if he claimed he wasn't so bad? So what if
he was still the sexiest damn cowboy she'd *ever* laid eyes on?

#506 SCANDALS JoAnn Ross

One night of fiery passion changed the lives of Bram Fortune and
Dani Cantrell forever. Grieving over the death of Bram's brother, who
was also her fiancé, Dani had turned to Bram. Six weeks later Dani
learned she was pregnant. Bram insisted they marry…but would Dani
ever stop loving his brother?

#507 PLAIN JANE'S MAN Kristine Rolofson

Plain Jane won a man. Well, not *exactly*. Jane Plainfield won a boat and
gorgeous Peter Johnson came with it. Jane hated the water, so what was
she going to do with the boat? Even worse, she had been badly burned
by romance—so what was she going to do with the man? Especially
when he wouldn't take *no* for an answer?

#508 STAR Janice Kaiser

Five years ago, Hollywood lured rising star Dina Winters. She
landed a movie deal, but left fiancé Michael Cross at the altar. Now
hotshot director Michael wants Dina for *his* movie. But she'll need an
Oscar-winning performance to work with the sexy man she never
stopped loving….

AVAILABLE NOW:

#501 GOLD AND GLITTER
Gina Wilkins
Lost Loves, Book 4

#502 WEDDING SONG
Vicki Lewis Thompson
Weddings, Inc.

#503 THE RANGER MAN
Sheryl Danson

#504 A TRUE BLUE KNIGHT
Roseanne Williams

MILLION DOLLAR SWEEPSTAKES (III)

No purchase necessary. To enter, follow the directions published. Method of entry may vary. For eligibility, entries must be received no later than March 31, 1996. No liability is assumed for printing errors, lost, late or misdirected entries. Odds of winning are determined by the number of eligible entries distributed and received. Prizewinners will be determined no later than June 30, 1996.

Sweepstakes open to residents of the U.S. (except Puerto Rico), Canada, Europe and Taiwan who are 18 years of age or older. All applicable laws and regulations apply. Sweepstakes offer void wherever prohibited by law. Values of all prizes are in U.S. currency. This sweepstakes is presented by Torstar Corp., its subsidiaries and affiliates, in conjunction with book, merchandise and/or product offerings. For a copy of the Official Rules send a self-addressed, stamped envelope (WA residents need not affix return postage) to: MILLION DOLLAR SWEEPSTAKES (III) Rules, P.O. Box 4573, Blair, NE 68009, USA.

EXTRA BONUS PRIZE DRAWING

No purchase necessary. The Extra Bonus Prize will be awarded in a random drawing to be conducted no later than 5/30/96 from among all entries received. To qualify, entries must be received by 3/31/96 and comply with published directions. Drawing open to residents of the U.S. (except Puerto Rico), Canada, Europe and Taiwan who are 18 years of age or older. All applicable laws and regulations apply; offer void wherever prohibited by law. Odds of winning are dependent upon number of eligibile entries received. Prize is valued in U.S. currency. The offer is presented by Torstar Corp., its subsidiaries and affiliates in conjunction with book, merchandise and/or product offering. For a copy of the Official Rules governing this sweepstakes, send a self-addressed, stamped envelope (WA residents need not affix return postage) to: Extra Bonus Prize Drawing Rules, P.O. Box 4590, Blair, NE 68009, USA.

SWP-H894

HARLEQUIN®

Temptation

Lost Loves

RIGHT MAN...WRONG TIME

Remember that one man who turned your world
upside down? Who made you experience all the
ecstatic highs of passion and lows of loss and regret.
What if you met him again?

You dared to lose your heart once and had it broken.
Dare you love again?

JoAnn Ross, Glenda Sanders, Rita Clay Estrada,
Gina Wilkins and Carin Rafferty. Find their stories in
Lost Loves, Temptation's newest miniseries, running
May to September 1994.

In September, experience EVEN COWBOYS GET
THE BLUES by Carin Rafferty. A one-night stand had
cost country-western hotshot Tanner Chapel plenty.
His marriage with Annie was over, his career was on
the skids and his dreams had begun to die. He wanted
Annie back...but could she learn to love and trust
again?

What if...?

LOST5

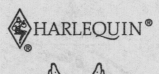

HARLEQUIN®

Weddings, Inc.

THE WEDDING GAMBLE
Muriel Jensen

Eternity, Massachusetts, was America's wedding
town. Paul Bertrand knew this better than
anyone—he never should have gotten soused at
his friend's rowdy bachelor party. Next morning
when he woke up, he found he'd somehow
managed to say "I do"—to the woman he'd
once jilted! And Christina Bowman had helped
launch so many honeymoons, she knew just
what to do on theirs!

THE WEDDING GAMBLE, available in
September from American Romance, is the
fourth book in Harlequin's new cross-line series,
WEDDINGS, INC.

Be sure to look for the fifth book,
THE VENGEFUL GROOM, by Sara Wood
(Harlequin Presents #1692), coming in October.

New York Times Bestselling Author

BARBARA DELINSKY

Look for her at your favorite retail outlet this September with

A SINGLE ROSE

A two-week Caribbean treasure hunt with rugged and sexy Noah VanBaar wasn't Shaye Burke's usual style. Stuck with Noah on a beat-up old sloop with no engine, she was left feeling both challenged and confused. Torn between passion and self-control, Shaye was afraid of being swept away by an all-consuming love.

Available in September, wherever Harlequin books are sold.

 HARLEQUIN®

BD2

This September, discover the fun of falling in love with...

love and laughter

Harlequin is pleased to bring you this exciting new collection of three original short stories by bestselling authors!

ELISE TITLE
BARBARA BRETTON
LASS SMALL

LOVE AND LAUGHTER—sexy, romantic, fun stories guaranteed to tickle your funny bone and fuel your fantasies!

Available in September wherever
Harlequin books are sold.

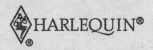

Fifty red-blooded, white-hot, true-blue hunks
from every State in the Union!

Look for MEN MADE IN AMERICA! Written by some of
our most popular authors, these stories feature fifty of
the strongest, sexiest men, each from a different state in
the union!

Two titles available every month at your favorite retail
outlet.

In August, look for:

PROS AND CONS by Bethany Campbell
(Massachusetts)
TO TAME A WOLF by Anne McAllister (Michigan)

In September, look for:

WINTER LADY by Janet Joyce (Minnesota)
AFTER THE STORM by Rebecca Flanders (Mississippi)

You won't be able to resist MEN MADE IN AMERICA!

HARLEQUIN®

Don't miss these Harlequin favorites by some of our most distinguished authors!
And now you can receive a discount by ordering two or more titles!

HT #25525	THE PERFECT HUSBAND by Kristine Rolofson	$2.99	☐
HT #25554	LOVERS' SECRETS by Glenda Sanders	$2.99	☐
HP #11577	THE STONE PRINCESS by Robyn Donald	$2.99	☐
HP #11554	SECRET ADMIRER by Susan Napier	$2.99	☐
HR #03277	THE LADY AND THE TOMCAT by Bethany Campbell	$2.99	☐
HR #03283	FOREIGN AFFAIR by Eva Rutland	$2.99	☐
HS #70529	KEEPING CHRISTMAS by Marisa Carroll	$3.39	☐
HS #70578	THE LAST BUCCANEER by Lynn Erickson	$3.50	☐
HI #22256	THRICE FAMILIAR by Caroline Burnes	$2.99	☐
HI #22238	PRESUMED GUILTY by Tess Gerritsen	$2.99	☐
HAR #16496	OH, YOU BEAUTIFUL DOLL by Judith Arnold	$3.50	☐
HAR #16510	WED AGAIN by Elda Minger	$3.50	☐
HH #28719	RACHEL by Lynda Trent	$3.99	☐
HH #28795	PIECES OF SKY by Marianne Willman	$3.99	☐

Harlequin Promotional Titles

#97122	LINGERING SHADOWS by Penny Jordan **(limited quantities available on certain titles)**	$5.99	☐

	AMOUNT	$
DEDUCT:	**10% DISCOUNT FOR 2+ BOOKS**	$
	POSTAGE & HANDLING	$
	($1.00 for one book, 50¢ for each additional)	
	APPLICABLE TAXES*	$_____
	TOTAL PAYABLE	$_____
	(check or money order—please do not send cash)	

To order, complete this form and send it, along with a check or money order for the total above, payable to Harlequin Books, to: **In the U.S.:** 3010 Walden Avenue, P.O. Box 9047, Buffalo, NY 14269-9047; **In Canada:** P.O. Box 613, Fort Erie, Ontario, L2A 5X3.

Name: _____

Address:_____City: _____

State/Prov.: _____ Zip/Postal Code: _____

*New York residents remit applicable sales taxes.
 Canadian residents remit applicable GST and provincial taxes..